CRITICS RECOMM

C000070158

"Jack Fritscher writes wonderful books."—*The Advocate*

"Describing Jack Fritscher as a writer of gay fiction is something akin to calling Duke Ellington a mere composer or Fred Astaire a mere dancer....Fritscher proves again why he's...'epicentric to gay literature'..., because he is a writer whose range, heat and intelligence...and wit are virtually unsurpassed in the genre....His trademarks are his erotic, inventive use of language, finely chiseled characters, and...diverse story settings....Jack Fritscher is...first and foremost an extraordinary American writer."
—Nancy Sundstrom, *Independent Publisher* Magazine

"Buckle your seatbelts and hang on...a fabulously authentic voice!"
—Lucie Jane Bledsoe, *Lambda Book Report*

"Erotic diversity. Sexual burn collides with sexual panic!"
—Tim Brough, *Vulcan* Magazine

"...bursting with plot, characters, energy, and ideas...Fritscher is as interested in gay history as the histrionics of gay relationships....he is unflinching and honest."   —Michael Bronski, *First Hand* Magazine

"...gritty, sexy, classic."   —Owen Keehnen, *Honcho*

"Literary...with enough wit to keep readers on their toes."
—*Gay Times*, London

Also by Jack Fritscher

Fiction

The Geography of Women
Rainbow County
Some Dance to Remember
Corporal in Charge
Stand by Your Man
Leather Blues

Non-Fiction

Mapplethorpe: Assault with a Deadly Camera
Popular Witchcraft
Love and Death in Tennessee Williams
When Malory Met Arthur: Camelot
Television Today

www.JackFritscher.com

Winged Victor

TITANIC
FORBIDDEN STORIES HOLLYWOOD FORGOT

Bon Voyage!

Jack Fritscher

Jack Fritscher

Palm Drive Publishing
San Francisco California

All *inquiries* concerning performance, adaptation, or publication rights should be addressed to Publisher, Palm Drive Publishing, PO Box 191021, San Francisco CA 94119. *Correspondence* may be sent to the same address. Send *reviews, quotation clips, feature articles, and academic papers* in hard copy, tear sheets, or electronic format for bibliographical inclusion on literary website and in actual archive.

For author history and literary research:
www.JackFritscher.com

Cover photograph, "Winged Victor," and all interior photographs,
        shot by and ©1999 Jack Fritscher
Cover design realized by Christine Dec Graphics, Sebastopol, California
Cover ©1999 Jack Fritscher

Palm Drive Publishing Literary Series 2006
Published by Palm Drive Publishing, P. O. Box 191021, San Francisco CA 94119
EMail: correspond@PalmDrivePublishing.com

Library of Congress Catalog Card Number: 98-89308
Fritscher, Jack 1939-
        Titanic: Forbidden Stories Hollywood Forgot / Jack Fritscher
        p. cm.
        ISBN 1-890834-30-0
        1. American Literature—20th Century. 2. Homosexuality—Fiction. 3. Gay
Studies—Fiction. 4. Erotica—Gay. 5. Sadomasochism—Fiction.

Printed in the United States of America
First Printing, January 1999
10 9 8 7 6 5 4 3 2 1

www.PalmDrivePublishing.com

For Mark Hemry,
editor, producer,
lover

CONTENTS

THE NOVELLA

THE SHORT STORIES

TALES FROM THE BEAR CULT

THE SCREENPLAY

That dark night on that cold, calm sea,
2,228 people watched *Titanic* go down:
228 were gay; 1,522 were in the water;
706 were in lifeboats.
The storytelling began...

JACK FRITSCHER'S
TITANIC!

Aboard *Titanic*. At sea. Westbound.
Wednesday, 10 April, 1912

Every night was a night to remember. The Astors had retired early from the grand first-class ballroom. So had the Rockefeller party. Edward Wedding, who was my lover since our second year at Oxford, sat next to me. He had excelled in sculling and sex while I, Michael Whitney, had distinguished myself with the British Romantic poets. And sex. Edward hated it when Mrs. Brown, who knew everything about everybody, teased him, calling him "Ever-Ready Eddy Weddy." She knew by looking, because Edward sported that certain look: the smug, engaging smile of a young man packing a big, how do you say in French, piece of pork.

Actually, we both had grown quite fond of Mrs. Brown who insisted she be called Molly. We three proved instantly agreeable tablemates the first day of the voyage as *Titanic* sailed proudly at noon from Southampton on April 10, Edward's twenty-sixth birthday. On *Titanic*'s brief stop at Queenstown, Ireland, Molly appreciated Edward's ship-rail comments about the hundreds of strapping young Irish tramping up the gangway to steerage, boys and girls immigrating to America's streets of gold. The shipboard gossip and salon *hauteur* was that Molly had been a showgirl, which was a scandal because showgirls, everyone knew, were always whores, no exceptions, thank you, even though Molly had married up into millions when she snagged the well-heeled land baron, the big-hung cowboy, Johnny Brown, back in Colorado.

Whatever she had been when she was on stage, Molly Brown was the kind of female who recognized two people in love, which, if it were two men, was aces by her. "Frankly, I prefer the company of you fellers. You know what you want when most don't. If love is what you got, you got more than the Astors. Besides, you dress better than the best, and you never laugh at any of my git-ups."

"Eddy Weddy," I said, "wants to wear your red ballgown with the red ostrich headdress." My American sense of sarcasm loved to pique Edward's British starch.

"Michael!" Edward said; no, Edward *commanded.* My dick stirred. His handsome jaw jutted out foursquare below his perfect white teeth and blond moustache. His eyes were bluer than the North Atlantic at high noon. His knee touched mine beneath the table. He had the strong body of a trained athlete. My cock rose thinking of his lean, hard thighs and long-muscled arms in his black cutaway. His tailor, lingering over measuring his long inseam, had commented how broad his sculling had made his shoulders, to say nothing, I mused, of his tight belly and mounded pecs, each crowned with a rosy brown nipple that grew hard when I sucked them and wet-rolled them between my fingers. His pecs and tits drove him crazy and made his big prick stand stalwart as a steel sword. As a coxswain to his crew, he was my cocksman in bed. "Michael," he repeated, "bugger off!"

Molly laughed in a tickling, tinkling cascade of feathers and diamonds and silk. This was our fifth night out, Sunday, on the magnificent ship. The eight-piece orchestra led swirling couples, colorful ladies held delicately by gentlemen in black, waltzing around and around the dance floor. "Everything smells so new," Molly said. "New wood. New paint. My new good fortune. And us new friends here, snug as bugs in a rug in the North Atlantic. I want it never to end!"

"Here, here." Edward said.

"All I want," Molly whispered, "is more ice in this fancy drink." She leered at Edward, waving her small hand, bejeweled with diamonds. "I simply adore big fat chunks of ice."

Four nights before, the very first night, Edward had asked our red-headed purser, Felix Jones, if rumor he had heard about the catwalks above and through the boiler rooms, and the hallways in the crew quarters in other ships was to be the case with *Titanic*.

"Cruising, you mean, sir?" Felix winked. "Why *Titanic*'s a cruise ship, isn't she now?"

"And the very fastest in the world," I said. "Top speed, 30 knots."

"Then," Felix said, "I suggest you young gentlemen head fast and quiet down the back stairs portside, say, about 11 o'clock. You'll find what you're looking for where the women never go. Some say first-class never mixes with second-class nor with steerage to say nothing of mixing after hours with the crew. What you see on your tickets, and what deck is your promenade, has no meaning below stairs. There's no distinctions down in the hold. Just men being men. Is there anything else I may do, gentlemen?" Felix was good-looking, a big-boned Welshman, no more than 22, our age, but we were reared worlds apart.

"Yes," Edward said. "Whom would you recommend?" He made a slow show of unbuttoning his shirt.

"Down below, sir?"

"Yes." He stripped off his shirt and stood magnificently buffed to the waist.

"I'm partial to the boiler-tenders, sir. The coal-heavers." The red-headed purser's face was flushing with sudden lust. "Shoveling coal night and day makes them strong."

"And dirty," I said.

"Which can be," Edward said, "a virtue."

"Why, Eddy," I said. I teased his aristocratic need for sexual slumming.

Felix was fully aroused and hardly at sixes and sevens about propriety in the suites he waited. His hard cock showed big in his black trousers. He was no small man, a good five-foot-ten, gifted with the body of his coal-miner father. He had worked in the mines of Wales as a boy and young man, and the work had made him strong. His tailored uniform could not disguise his deep-chest, tight biceps, moon rump, and thick thighs that left no room for his hardening cock to be decent in a first-class suite.

I could see in his green eyes the cautious, yet confident, look the lower classes have, because they know they're what the upper classes seek most when they slip out on the slum. In heaven or hell, or on the water, there's nothing more attractive to a rich man than a lower-class stud, even one bettering himself by choosing to be a purser rather than a shoveler in the boiler room. Felix Jones had had enough of coal in Wales. On the high seas, he had a taste for serving young gentlemen.

Edward took a step toward Felix, reached around him, locked the door, and groped his hand along the shiny length of the well-trained purser's untrained, hard cock. Felix's head rolled back on his strong neck. I unbuttoned his shirt and brushed my nose through the surprise of thick red hair covering his chest, licking into his sweat-sweet armpits, and tonguing his nipples.

Edward unbuttoned the man's trousers, springing out a 9-inch cock, the alabaster white kind twined with thick blue veins peculiar to translucent penises rooted in a thatch of hickory-red hair. We were all three quickly stripped naked as the Queen's Guard at bath call. Edward fell to his knees sucking Felix's thick shaft, no gagging or gurgling, merely smooth moves, sliding his face down on the purser's hard cock, as naturally as he had taken to the long oar in sculling on the Thames where I had only dared punt.

I stood on the bed and shoved my fat dick down the redhead's mouth, glorying in the sensation of his thick red moustache bristling, brushing my cock topside. With

my hands, I played their four tits like a bumblebee con-
certo for twin pianos. Edward pumped his long, sleek,
thoroughbred horsecock with his hand, the way he preferred to control his cuming, unless it was, as it had
usually been from the start, shoved up my ass the way
he'd first reamed my hole with his long rod the rainy
Oxford afternoon we'd met at the foot of Christopher
Wren's Tom Tower in the great quad of Christ Church.

His 10-inch cock for the first three months was 3
inches too big for me, and then, suddenly, he said he loved
me, and my cheeks spread, my hole opened up, and he
drove his 10 inches to the hilt deep into me. Light, blinding as dawn piercing a rose window, illuminated me from
my asshole to my head. The best measure of any big
cock's true length and width and volume is the measure
a man makes of it clamped deep inside his butthole. Vlad
the Impaler had nothing on Edward Wedding. "And I love
you," I said.

Edward's forceful sucking was too much for Felix
Jones who had never been throated so skillfully in all his
life in Wales. As he began to cum, he began to shout. He
was really quite amusing. To silence him, I screwed my
own cock down his face as far as I could thread my thick
8-inch piece of Boston pipe. My cum burst down so deep
inside him, his shouting turned to moaning. Cum spurt-
ed from his nose and his mouth. His tongue licked clots
of hot white seed from his red moustache, and his green
eyes widened in a kind of awed gratitude. (I like to think.)
The sight and feel of dripping cum and spit, mixed with
my telling Felix to grab hold of Edward's tits and squeeze-
roll them as tight as he could, caused my masturbating
Edward to shoot the load from his 10-inch cannon all

across the new rose carpet of *Titanic*.

Maniacs, we fell in a tangle, in a peerage of sex, upon one of the single beds, all three of us, equal, grown young men, in a sweaty pant, huffing and puffing, laughing and eating cum from fingers and chests and moustaches and flopping wet cocks. Edward was so jolly. He lifted Felix's perfect redhead's dick, its thickness in sausage proportion to its length.

"You, Felix, are truly titanic!"

He broke out three cigars and we lay abed, smoking peacefully, talking and cuddling, comparing cocks, and doing everything *encore*, on that our first night at sea as *Titanic* sped through the dark waters of the North Atlantic, toward America, toward New York, toward home.

"*Titanic*," Molly Brown asked. "What does it mean?"

"The Titans were rebellious gods who were too big for their britches," Edward said. "They wished to overturn the established order."

"Good for them," Molly said.

"I think rather," I said, "the ship is named for Titania."

"Who's she?" Molly asked. "Should I meet her?"

"She's the queen of the faeries," Edward said. "Shakespeare." Edward was evening the score for my teasing him. "You already know her, but her name this time is Michael." He pointed at me.

"Then, Michael," Molly said, "I add you to the list of royalty of my recent acquaintance."

"Queen Michael," Edward said, working his vengeance on me for laughing at Molly's dubbing him "Eddy Weddy."

"Don't be ridiculous," I said. "No man should ever be called a queen."

"Some men should," Edward said.

Molly pealed with laughter. I'd have punched her, but she was a suffragette and I heard they punched back.

"May this then," Edward said, raising his glass in a champagne toast, "be the start of a great tradition." He grinned. "To Queen Michael!"

"I'll drink to that," Molly said. "To Queen Michael."

Decorum overcame my anger at the feminine suggestion. In America, I had worked since boyhood to make my gestures and voice as masculine as my body, and found in England less pressure for a comfortable compromise. "Ha!" I said, "Ah-ha!" I lifted my own glass. No better way to squelch a joke than to join it. "To Queen Michael," I said, "and don't you, my subjects, forget it." I snatched Molly's diamond tiara from her head and crowned myself. They all laughed.

"Keep it," Molly said. "That glass looks better on you than it does on me." "That glass" was twenty-two 10-carat Hapsburg diamonds. "Sooner or later everyone needs a tiara, my dear. You may need it someday." She put her hand on mine. "My sweet young man, let Molly bring you luck."

The second night out, promptly at 11, Felix led us down five flights of backstairs to the hold. The noise of the engines, only a purr in our stateroom, drowned out the sound way above of the orchestra playing the "Varsouviana." The roaring, revolving engines drove their long steel pistons deep into *Titanic*'s guts like huge copulation machines. The maze of catwalks was lined at both rails with sailors, coalmen, cooks, mechanics, and blackamoor masseurs from the Turkish steam room. The hot red tips of the crewmen's rolled cigarettes and the gentlemen's cigars blinked with each drag in the dark like stars signaling in the night. We threaded our way through the silent, standing men, taking our bearings.

"I leave you gentlemen here," Felix said. "They look rough. They are rough, most of them, some of them, no doubt, criminals, but they know where they are. *Titanic* is their discipline. They must be careful with nowhere to escape but the open sea. So you are safe. Perfect, yes? They know you are not them. The same as you gentlemen, they have their terms. They want at night only what they give you by day. Service." He turned, then turned back. "Enjoy yourselves, gentlemen." He disappeared through the lounging lines of men standing in the half-darkness of the red bulbs lighting the engine room.

"Let's take an adventure," Edward said. "Let's split up."

"Divide and conquer."

He put his arms around me, even surrounded as we were by so many dark eyes in the red glow. "I love you," he said.

"I love you," I said. "More than life itself."

"Ah," he said, "but not more than all this irresistible cock."

"Let's regroup at our suite."

"When?"

"Whenever."

"Our clock is not ticking."

"Time is not running out on us. We have a week to kill on this voyage."

We parted company and I cruised out on my own,

slowly strolling down the catwalk, eyeing the sailors and laborers, growing bolder with each step, stopping, staring, eye-to-eye, measuring my choice. *Titanic* was like half of Noah's ark: there was one of every kind.

A hand pulled on my trousers. I looked down at a blond lad with the face of an orphaned angel. "Take me, sir. Only one quid."

"No one told me anyone charged by the 'pound' down below," I said.

"I do, sir."

He was a ragamuffin cabin boy. His confident smile told me he usually received what he asked for.

"All right then, first tell me how big you are."

"Fourteen, sir."

"Fourteen inches? My! My! Then you are worth something."

"No, sir. Fourteen years. Next month."

"Sorry, my boy. I'm looking for beef not chicken."

"I need the money for my sick mother back in Liverpool."

"You have the stench of an orphanage about you."

"Nossir. I mean, yessir, but I seen you above deck and you looked..."

"Like a mark."

"Yessir. You all look, forgive me, sir, like marks to a lad like me."

"Here." I laid a sovereign in his soft hand. "The money's for you, not your mother, isn't it?"

"Who else, sir? My mother's been dead long since I was born. Eighteen years ago."

Of legal age, but selling his wares as a "young boy," off he ran into the darkness. I wondered at the justice in the world where the B Deck middle-class was chained off at the stairs leading to first-class of A Deck, and steerage was caged off, lower down on C Deck, to keep them from reaching middle-class. *Titanic* was a true social microcosm. Ah, well, perhaps my small donation to the lad would bring me luck with a bruiser of a man.

I grew bolder. A sailor, blond-bearded, short and barrel-chested, stood insouciant against the rail, his white uniform bright in the dark. The flap of his trousers was unbuttoned. His huge cock hung an easy 8 inches soft against the down-turned flap. I walked up to him and touched his beautiful blond beard. He smiled and sucked my finger into his mouth with his hot wet tongue. I made love to his bristled face, raking his beard with my teeth, sucking it with my lips. I dropped one hand to his cock. The soft, foreskin-hooded, fat shaft began to rise hydraulically.

"Suck me," he said.

I looked left and right. Everywhere men were tangled up. No rules applied below deck. I fell to my knees, tonguing and lipping the tip of his cock.

"I said, *suck me*." His voice rose deep from his big hairy balls.

I slid down his uncircumcised cock. He reached down and unbuttoned my shirt, feeling for my nipples. His slowly engorging cock hung soft as a long fat slug waiting for me to suck its 8 inches up to 10. Its skin was blond-baby soft, softer than velvet. It rolled to the left of his groin, hardening under my study. Alive. Pulsing. Its color in the red light was that fresh-meat pink peculiar to blond dicks. He flexed his tool like a muscle. It bounced and rolled. The cockhead peered like an eye from the circling lid of foreskin. He smelled clean enough, and nasty enough. I took his meat in my hand and licked my forefinger, inserting it inside his foreskin, circling its big mushroom head, feeling clots of cheese scoop ahead of my finger. I pulled out and looked at his smegma, an *hors d'oeuvre* sweeter than any first-class buffet could provide.

"You too good for that, sir?" Disdain tinted his voice.

"I, sir," deliberately throwing the term back to him to show him he was boss, "live for such delicacy."

"Then gi' me the pleasure to see you eat it."

The thick clot of blond cheese was tastier than Danish brie. I rolled it like a connoisseur on my tongue, sucked it through my teeth, wanting the taste of him in my mouth to linger strong when next I kissed Edward, himself out harvesting the juice of men for me.

"Show it to me on your tongue," he ordered.

I opened my mouth and held out my tongue. He smiled, and dropped a long, thick strand of spit directly from his mouth to mine.

"Mix it up and swallow the pud," he said. His cock was rising by degrees, like some leviathan from the dark sea. He enjoyed toying with men like me who like to be the toys of men like him.

I squished his cheese and spit, mixing it into a heaven-sent *paté*, Smacking my lips to please him.

"Swallow it," he said.

I savored one last taste and gulped his juices down my throat.

His cock stood at hard attention, its head still shrouded by its cowl of foreskin.

"Peel me back," he said. "With your tongue."

I worked my tongue across his big piss-slit and into

his foreskin, finding more of his cheese, swallowing it, wrapping both my hands around his hard cock, pulling the skin of the shaft down, popping the huge mushroom head of his enormous cock free of the envelope of his foreskin.

"Suck me." He said it the way I'm sure he said it to Amsterdam whores. I could tell that his cock was the center of his blond, bearded, well-built being. He had the ruggedly handsome look of a man who always got what he wanted sexually.

With no trouble at all.

Especially from me. I took the bulbous head of his dick into my mouth. Its hard volume plugged my face. I worked his uncut head in and out. His fully stiff cock stood the length of my two handsful between my crossed eyes. He was a choker. He knew it. He liked it. My tongue fucked his piss-slit. He moaned. I bit lightly on his head. He moaned louder. I chewed the head of his cock. He slapped the side of my head with his calloused hand.

"Suck me," he commanded. "Go down on me." A litany of profanity spilled out. "Swallow my big hard blond cock all the way down your bloody throat till you feel the bloody hairs in my crotch scratch your bloody nose."

I obeyed. I took him inch by inch, swallowing, savoring slowly the masculine taste and soft skin of his strong cock.

"I said, *suck it!*" He liked fast, robust sucks. He put his giant hands on the back of my head, curled his tough fingers into my hair, and jammed me into a nose-dive down to the base of his steel rod. In and out, working his dick like the pistons ramming *Titanic* engines, battering my throat, tears watering from my eyes, spit and cock-juice drooling from my mouth, my nose foaming, my voice choked to groaning that grew louder the harder he fucked my face. His demands, commands, in abandon, turned to snarls and grunts. He plugged the O-ring at the back of my mouth, the final ring that leads down the throat, with his mushroom head. I whipped my own cock to a frenzy as he drove me, kneeling, and bent me over backwards, till he had lowered me flat to the catwalk and straddled me. Never once did his cock leave my face, even as he fell to his knees and, pumping push ups, drilled me deep, pulling almost out past my sucking, begging lips.

What a common uncommon sight we must have made! Feet and legs gathered in a circle three deep around us. Dark shadows of men stroking their cocks watched the wild show of his wild fuck of my face. His rams became stronger, faster, more urgent. The crotch flap of his whites whipped my chest, exciting my nipples. My cock was mine. He cared nothing about it juicing in my fist. I reached both my palms up to cup his perfect butt through his white sailor cloth, but he bucked my hands off, muttering, "My ass is mine! Eat my cock, you fucking cocksucker!"

Men, staying well out of the muscular blond sailor's way, fell to their knees in a circle around my head lying on the catwalk floor. Cocks of every size and shape shot their loads on my face. I was drowning in sperm. The more he fucked, the more shooting cocks replaced shooting cocks. My hair matted with anonymous cum. My throat ached with his ramming. My cock pitched to the breach of cuming. He lunged. He roared up his full height on his knees: his big wet dick, swung free from my mouth, red with heat, flailing in the air, searching like a lost ship

for the port of my mouth. He swore. He cursed. He blas-
phemed. He took his raging dick in both his meathooks
and plunged it one last time so far down my throat I
feared his load might shoot out my ass. Again, he withdrew, this time a slow suctioning pump, sump-pumping
himself up to his final blast, pulling his pole, inch by inch,
from my mouth and kneeling across my chest, raising his
arms out sideways from his muscular hips, crooked forward at the elbow, his hands fists, mighty above my face,
and with a roar that started in his balls, shot up his spine,
hit his head, shot again back down his spine to his balls,
he exploded long aerial flumes of white sperm across my
face, with me cuming in my own hand, my mouth open,
swallowing, eating his load, eating the dozen other loads
of men whose cocks he triggered by his big shoot.

Upstairs in the Main Salon, Molly Brown was dragging a reluctant table or two of reticent rich into a chorus of the popular "Meet Me in St. Louis, Louis." Edward
was by her side. His evening had been fun, if not tame,
and he had spent an hour with Madame Ouspenskaya
whose unsettling reading of his Tarot he was trying to
forget.

"I saw you," he said, in our stateroom. "You were
disgusting."

"Yes," I said. "I know."

He grinned. "Let me lick all that cum from your face
and your hair." He pulled out his hardening cock.

"And we still have three glorious nights to go before *Titanic* docks in New York."

Aboard *Titanic*. At sea. Westbound.
Friday, 12 April, 1912

Travel heightens observation. One remembers details, impressions, feelings. The Ryersons spoke to the Astors and the Astors spoke only to God knows. Poor Molly Brown, dragged up in her feathers and boas with a fat purse bulging with new cash, couldn't truly jolly her way into that tightest of first circles. If it wasn't her clothes she tripped on, it was her brash sense of Colorado humor. "I'm just you before you married a bank account," she said to Mrs. Leland-Wynston. Maggie came on like a hatpin in a salon stuffed with balloons filled with hot air. The rich prefer to buy their jesters, safe clowns, not pointed wits like dear sweet Molly.

Edward and I escorted the redoubtable Mrs. Brown for a brisk walk on deck. The sea was calm. The stars were brighter than ever I'd seen.

"First-class is such a bore," Molly said. "No wonder you boys disappear early every evening leaving me alone with that little pack of Spanish gigolos. I swear they boarded with nothing but their Brilliantine hair tonic and their tuxedos with empty pockets hoping to earn their way by dancing horizontal tangos across the North Atlantic. By God! I've never paid for it. Although I have been paid."

"Why, Molly," Edward said. "How droll."

"Eddy Weddy," Molly stopped us dead in our tracks. "Do I for one minute look...*droll?*"

"Molly, you always look wonderful," I said.

"Thank you, kind sir." She patted her hourglass figure. "I have appeared on the stage," she said. "Make of that what you will. Everyone else seems to."

"I apologize," Edward said.

"Don't be an ass," Molly said. She took us both by the arm and like a decorated tugboat steered us toward the prow of the ship.

"The night is lovely." I tried to make conversation.

Two decks below us, a piano and concertinas and tin whistles rose in harmony with the gales of Irish laughter of the hundreds of passengers dancing and singing in steerage. We peered over the railing. The sight was sweet. Young couples held each other close. A young father danced with his two infant sons in his arms while his wife, all of them looking straight from County Cork, danced with him, her arms outstretched to his waist, circling in her family. The dance floor was circled by men waiting their turn to catch some idle girl. Even the homeliest would do. The men in steerage outnumbered the women six to one.

"So this is what the simple folk do," Edward said.

"Don't be a snob," Molly said. She turned an inquisitive glance on both Edward and me. "What do these men do?"

Edward and I broke into laughter.

"That's what I thought," Molly said. "Stop laughing and tell me. I left Colorado to find out everything about the world."

Needless to say, Molly got an earful, though Edward was too much the gentleman to distress her with certain facts, or worse, certain rumors. *Titanic,* some said, was built so fast by its construction crew, welding massive iron plates, driven to even speedier work by investors, that stories spread that laborers who lagged behind were welded up alive, abandoned and forgotten inside *Titanic*'s giant echoing bulkheads.

Edward, ever polite, delivered Molly the superficial truth, as glycerine-smooth as the waters of the North Atlantic sea spread so flat and calm as far as we could see. I, ever the literature scholar, could have told her the same tale, but more like Chaucer, deeper, "The Stoker's Tale," deep as the sea we skimmed across, deep as the dark hold was below the glimmering lights of the Grand Ballroom where the band played on, all of us pilgrims to Canterbury. Voyeur that I am, I had followed Edward down below deck. I knew how he was when he was with me. I wondered how he was with other men.

Edward's 10-inch cock drew men like magnets; but Edward, for all his aristocratic distinction, was fickle as everyone else. No matter how big one's own cock, the search is always for a man whose cock is bigger. "The hung don't care to fuck down." Edward had once said that.

"But I," I said, "have only 8. That's 1 inch for each of my 8 million bucks when daddy dies."

That made him laugh and grow tender. "But you I love," he said. "When I go slumming, that's a different story."

Love and slumming.

I spied the man even before Edward. I knew his taste for the heroic. The giant stood in the shadows, a coal-heaver, a stoker, stripped to the waist, his chest and shoulders as magnificent as his powerful arms. His face was the kind of rugged brute handsome that makes dicks rise. His tousled hair and short beard were black as the coal-grime covering him from head to foot. Even so, his nipples jutted prominent from his pectorals, nipples almost pink in the red lights of the hold, as if he had licked his dirty fingers and tweaked them clean. His hands, like his hairy forearms, were massive from heavy labor.

I could only guess, as could Edward, what all this upper-body promise meant below his carved waist, cinched tight with a rope holding up his coal-heaver's blackened leather pants. His big feet, spread wide in black boots, formed a triangle up to his crotch where the leather barely concealed the thickness of his long driving ram. He was an animal, born so, the kind of man rich men hire to power their empires, their factories, their ships.

He was, I sensed, the man who made *Titanic* go.

He waited as if he knew Edward was advancing toward him and him alone. He groped his huge crotch. He groaned deep from his big balls. His lips parted the dark thatch of his short, rugged beard. His white teeth shone, not in smile, but in heat. Men kept their distance. He towered well over 6-3 and weighed in at a hard-packed good 265. He was a Goliath, perfect for *Titanic*. Perfect for Edward. Actually, perfect for me. For the first time, I felt a fleeting, just fleeting, twinge of jealousy. It wasn't I didn't want Edward to have him. It was more I wanted him too, but that, as it turned out, was never to be.

Edward walked straight up within three paces of the Stoker. Each surveyed the other. Edward's hard, lean-muscled body looked good to me in the dim red light. He pulled off his shirt, exposing his sculler's chest and broad shoulders. The two men stood stripped to the waist, squared off, stanced like men who are about to make love like fighters. The Stoker raised both his massive arms, flexing them the way I had seen Mr. Sandow exhibit his biceps in a gentlemen's salon in London. Eugen Sandow, having set the fashion for physique posing, would have fled back to Germany had he seen the Stoker's arms, his sweaty armpits, and the twin mountains of his nipple-crowned chest. He lowered his challenging arms and stroked one hand across his hairy pectorals and down his sculpted hairy belly, stopping only when his big hand cupped his crotch.

Edward reached for his wallet and placed a hundred pound note on a box halfway between them.

The Stoker nudged a coal-heaver next to him who picked up the bill. "That's for what hardness you seen," the Stoker said. His accent was Czech, but his English was clear. "What else depends."

"Depends on what?" Edward, ever undaunted, was especially bold with a hardon.

"Depends on what you got." He groped his grimy crotch, bouncing his almost visible cock and balls. "Depends on what you want."

The surrounding coal-heavers and more than several slumming gentlemen laughed.

Like a gambler with an ace in the hole, Edward palmed his hard 10-inch cock, exhibiting its outline in his trousers.

The laughter stopped dead in the water.

Except for the Stoker. "I eat that for snack."

Edward was expert at fencing. He took a step forward, closing the distance between them, and parried.

He pointed at the Stoker's crotch. "I eat that for another hundred pounds."

"Crazy rich Britisher boy," the Stoker said. "You will eat my whole focking body before you eat my big focking cock."

He raised his arm, exposing his wet armpit. I nearly swooned from the rich sweet smell of his body. Edward took the last step in. The Stoker took him with one hand on the back of his head and pushed his face into the sweaty, muscled tangle of long black hair. Edward, Molly's "Ever-ready Eddy Weddy," landed willingly, tongue-first in the Stoker's armpit. He made sucking, slurping sounds that made my cock hard.

I wasn't the first man, coal-heaver or gentleman, all equal voyeurs, who pulled my cock from my trousers to stroke along with their rugged foreplay. Edward and the Stoker stopped all the other action in the vicinity dead in its tracks, just like the couple on a dance floor who are so good all the other dancers stop in a sophisticated circle to watch and applaud. I knew Edward loved theatre, but I'd never known him to give a performance.

I knew we'd both remember this little show till the day we died.

The Stoker, with one strong hand, moved Edward from one armpit to the other, dragging his wet and willing tongue through the thick hair on his chest, hair matted like seaweed around the aureole islands of his big leather-tough nipples. His muscular arm bulged. Huge veins, heated with hard work and stoked with passion, coiled like snakes through the black hair furzing his biceps and hamhock forearm. No doubt his cock was even more thick-veined.

He guided Edward's sweaty blond moustache and licking tongue up to his dark beard. "Chew it! Eat it!"

Edward slurped the sweatsalt from the Stoker's coarse beard. Tight curly black hairs caught in his teeth. He chewed like the challenger he was and came at the coalman full force, following the dance, but never giving an inch. The tougher the Stoker got, the rougher Edward responded. I thought I could see in the Stoker's eyes a hint of dumb surprise. Few men, if any, ever gave him what he wanted much less upped the ante.

He yanked Edward back by the hair, held his head six inches from his face, and stared at him eye to eye, man to man, sizing up this startling young gentleman athlete the way Goliath must have looked at the young David standing defiant with a rock in his hand.

He spit, a long white flume of spit, into Edward's face.

Edward spit it back. And grinned.

The Stoker's breath was as sweet as when he had been a muscular boy harvesting the hay fields of Czechoslovakia. He was younger by ten years than his huge size made him look. With Edward's spit hanging like white cum in his black beard, he was no more than 30, but his command presence made him seem like an ancient god.

They stood frozen in the circle of masturbating cocks. The Stoker laughed, broke the *tableau*, and from his laughing mouth, in the distorted shadows of the red light, his tongue, long and tubular inched slowly from between his lips, the head of it, swear to God, looked in the brilliant darkness like nothing so much as the head of a Roman-orgy cock, the way the sides rolled up, forming a piss-slit, the shaft of it coming out hard as a dick, slow inch by slow inch, the blue veins stark, mean, the volume tumescent, sticking out big and hard, a cocklike blowgun bulleting out thick white clots of spit rapid as a Gatling gun, targeting Edward's open mouth, a foaming pool of the Stoker's sweet cumlike juice.

Edward, not to be outdone, spit the load back on the Stoker's greasy chest, white-hot lather mixing into the thick black hair forested across the big man's high, wide, and handsome pecs.

That did it.

The Stoker drove his 5-inch tongue, mushroomhead and shaft, straight through Edward's lips and deep into the back of his mouth, tongue-fucking him hard as any cock, hawking his spermy spit back into his throat, shooting the cum of his spit into Edward's guts.

All this presentation of credentials, two stags squared off, took all of six minutes. The rest took longer.

Edward rebelliously jerked his hair loose from the Stoker's grip. He popped open his trousers, dropped his shorts, and displayed his 10-inch rockhard cock. Three masturbating bystanders, two lords, and one lord who was a lady trapped in a lord's body, shot their loads on the spot. Edward wrapped both his hands, big-boned from rowing team, around his shaft, squeezing the angry purple head of his dick to plum-size. He grinned his challenge, then spit his own spit splatdown on the leather crotch of the Stoker's tentpoled pants.

The Stoker growled.

There was ass on the line.

The crowd howled.

The Stoker slowly unbuttoned his leathers. He

teased a gruff tease like some primal folkdance. Anticipation in the circle of voyeurs grew. His hairy white
thighs, untouched by coal-grime, glowed with sweat in
the red light.

His dick was so long and so hard, it hung like a
galvanized pipe three-quarters of the way down his thigh.
The man was hung with a horsecock crossbred with bull
balls. A groan, a sigh, and slight applause rose from the
audience who'd given up betting for masturbating. It was
obvious. Edward and the Stoker, two different classes of
men, were as perfect an odds-on match as *Titanic* was
for the North Atlantic.

"When I beat you, young gentleman, sir," the Stoker said. He appreciated Edward's cock and cockiness.
"You will stay with me for 24 focking hours below decks
in the hold, in the boiler room, maybe even in chains in
the brig, just so you see, young gentleman, how men like
you make men like us live."

Edward, ever the knightly aristocrat, picked up the
gauntlet. He hated socialism and bolshevism; he took on
the Stoker's dare as if the laborer were the devil Trotsky
himself. As an American man, matched, mmm, "married," in great subtlety, to a bit of a British snob, I had to
listen at tea to such lordly politics with feigned sympa-
thy, when, I, like Molly Brown, much preferred the social leveling of the bedroom where everyone, Astor and
Guggenheim, ends up horizontal, even as, I bet, Trotsky
himself, with his legs in the air.

How could Edward not win for losing on the Stoker's dare? Edward either took the Stoker's 14-fat-inches
down his throat, and, mind you, up his ass, or he had to
spend a day and a night in the hold getting up to the

Stoker's "focking" speed, outdistancing his old sculling records, the way *Titanic*, slicing through the still, cold waters was outdistancing itself and her sister ship, *Olympic*.

The Stoker stripped naked to his boots. Edward shucked his clothes and shoes. A sailor started rapping a rhythmic tattoo on the iron railing in time to the rods pistoning the huge engines. The Stoker was a stroker, wrapping both big hands around his cock, squeezing out a third handful, vein-popping the bulbous mushroom head, its piss-slit dripping translucent 40-weight lube webs. His was a savage cock, primitive, animal, evolved somehow, from the mountain giants of Eastern Europe into a steel-hard, mechanized piston. The way his ox-driving ancestors wielded their barbarian swords, the Stoker aimed his ram at Edward like some unspeakable industrial weapon.

I fairly swooned.

Lucky Eddy Weddy. Was he ever ready for this?

Oh, my, yes. The Stoker, I knew, was the stuff of Edward's dreams. No matter his politics.

No sooner did I take my own hard cock in my hand than a handsome young sailor, blond as Melville's angelic Billy Budd, dived mouth-first on it, freeing me to grope the cocks standing hard out all about us, every eye fixed on the Stoker, double-fisting his animal cock. Edward, who knelt only to royalty, recognized the regal superiority of the noble savage, and fell to his knees, his own 10-inch cock stiff enough to fly the colors, his mouth open as wide as a choir boy stuck on the jaw-dropping fourth note of "Oh, Holy Night."

The Stoker roared.

The crowd roared.

Titanic roared.

I feared for Edward's life and limb, but I knew he'd die a happy death with his limbs all over the place. Slowly, savoring his dripping gusto, the Stoker drove the full circumference of his dickhead into Edward's open mouth, hungry for the only thing he had ever hungered for in all his privileged life. First-class dining was not upstairs. Downstairs, real life teemed.

The Stoker's roar caused two men boxing hardon-naked fifty feet away to stop their bare-knuckle fisticuffs.

Edward ate the apple-sized dickhead like Adam swallowing in Eden. He dropped his jaw, fearful of scraping the giant's meat. The Stoker's hairy body flexed, driving his fist-dick in short, quick jabs and longer punches deeper into Edward's salivating mouth. Spit and sweat and lube dripped shiny down Edward's fine pectorals and belly. He put his hands on the Stoker's huge thighs.

"You like my focking, uh?" He finger-locked his thick hands around Edward's head, hands so big I could see only Edward's nose and his straining mouth as the Stoker drove inch upon inch of his battering ram, in, into Edward, always in, never pulling back an inch, choke-fucking his face, pulling finally back, pumping in and out, teasing open the back of Edward's mouth, the top of the tunnel of his throat, the hot, wet, tight throat where the Stoker aimed to plant the root of his cock that no man had ever swallowed whole before.

If a man has moments, Edward, I knew, kneeling between the grimy Stoker's legs, was having a night to remember all his life. My own cock was so close to cuming, I pulled the blond sailor off my dick and set him to work on my balls. Almost instantly, that triggered him. He rose up, a handsome devil, brandishing his long, hard cock, and shot ropes of white sperm up my belly. As soon as he came, he was gone. Another sailor dived on my dick. I guided him to my nuts. Other hands, other tongues licked cum from my torso. In the hot sea of sex surging about me, I thanked God I was tall. I wanted to be head and shoulders above them all so not to lose the vision of the Stoker's dick, obscenely white against his coal-skin, pistoning Edward's mouth. Edward always swallowed my 8-inches easily, and the Stoker had an easy 8 inches snaked down his throat. Edward, ever the sexual athlete, ever wanting *more*, was face-to-face with *more*. The Stoker had plumbed his throat with his first 8-inches and had 6 inches more of thick, hard cock to drive home.

I thought to call a halt, but in the dark night of the hold, the fires blazing in the furnaces, I knew what would seem in first-class as brutality was in truth the intense engagement of two men locked in sexual ritual older than prehistory, older than the gods, older than the Titans themselves. Besides, Edward was a strong, athletic sportsman who knew how to handle himself. He hardly needed me to climb through the invisible ropes of the invisible ring to referee a stop to the match.

For a moment, I saw his eyes, staring, between the Stoker's arms, down the fat 6-inch tube of remaining cock, determined to bury his nose in the muscular giant's curling crotch hair or die trying. Something, a lightning, as much lust as courage, flashed in his eyes. He gulped. The Stoker, not insensitive, drove a 9th inch slowly down into Edward.

Something clicked between them.

The Stoker seemed suddenly almost tender. More than he wanted to "fock" Edward by storm, he wanted someone to finally, really, totally swallow his 14-inch cock, to set an all-time land-sea record. Perhaps he sensed in Edward's willingness his chance, at last, to feel teeth and lips, chewing and sucking, at the big base of his cockroot. He oozed the 10th iron-hard inch down.

The crowd called out for more. A chant rose up. Pipes banged rhythmically. Money changed hands. Cocks rose up. Men shouted. Cuming. Sucking. Fucking. Watching. Shooting.

The Stoker and Edward both, a pair now, rose to the moment. I think Edward's throat actually opened an inch farther and literally suctioned the Stoker's 11th inch in so fast, the facefucker was jolted almost out of his big boots with surprise.

Edward had taken the offensive.

A grin broke through the Stoker's brute-handsome face. He had that space between his two solid front teeth that I've often found to be characteristic of truly aggressive sexual men. He took hardon pleasure in Edward's attack and sworded the challenge of his 12th inch, a foot of cock, down Edward's throat. It all happened so slow, so easy, almost so delicately, that I hardly noticed that Edward, whose goal in life had long been 12 inches, had swooned, fainted, passed out. Smiling in victory.

What to do? I pushed the suckers and lickers away from my cock and balls and tits and asshole. The crowd was too thick for me to make it the five feet to Edward impaled, hanging, jaw ajut, on the huge steel-hard cock. I shouldn't have worried. Felix Jones, our red-headed purser, had told us no harm could happen below decks.

The Stoker himself, like the coal boss he was, flexed his massive body, establishing his command presence, and, like a conqueror barbarian, lifted Edward gently up, suctioning his dick out of Edward's throat, vacuuming up, popping finally the deep probe of his cockhead from Edward's grinning lips. His eyes fluttered open.

"Am I dead?" he asked.

"Not yet," the Stoker said.

"Good," Edward said. He spoke like a drunk happy on champagne. "We have another 2 inches to go."

"Focker!" the Stoker said. "But we reverse engines."

Bodily, he lifted Edward like a doll in his big-muscled arms above his head. His huge cock staffed its full 14 inches straight up 80-degrees dead ahead. Without so much as a quiver in his massive shoulders and chest and legs, he held Edward, his big hands in his armpits, his gnarled thumbs on his lean chest, like a conquered toy soldier above his head. The Stoker's cock drooled shine. His dick was a bulkhead as magnificent as *Titanic*'s jutting straight up, so erect its very skin stretched paper-thin over its ropes of veins and sinew. The tip of his cockhead, poised, waiting, drooling, dripping, flexing, like a ram awaiting its target to come bulls-eye to it.

I didn't need Mr. Muybridge to get the picture.

The still *tableau* of this *pas de deux* froze in the red-dark of the hold for an eternity of seconds. The crowd fell back, then forward, a hundred hard cocks masturbating at the sight, shooting up at them like flares in the night signaling the collision as the Stoker, slowly lowered Edward, ass-first, down through the arc of distance to the ice-hard head of his steaming cock.

The Stoker guided Edward's tight butthole straight

down his slippery dick, its head popping the rim of Edward's skilled ass-ring, snaking, serpentine, deeper into Edward's ass, both of them roaring, each man making a match for the other, two animals locked in heat, flames from the belching furnaces lighting them, fucking like demons in the hot bowels of Hades.

The Stoker's steady cock was 7, then 8, then 9 inches plumb-deep in Edward's trembling body as their faces passed, longitude and latitude. The Stoker held Edward eye-to-eye.

"I fock you now."

"Fock me!" A beast inside my civilized Edward shouted.

A large bead of envy surged to the head of my engorged cock. Never had I conjured such lust in him; but my heart was glad he had found it in his daring self.

The Stoker, sweat running rivers from his armpits, grunted. His square teeth, separate as short pickets, grinned.

Edward grinned back. "Fock me!"

The Stoker spit a flume as white as cum.

Edward's face dripped. "Fock me!"

The Stoker slipped his big hands up Edward's raised arms, dropping him down on the 14-inch ram of his cock. Fully impaled, Edward roared with the beginning of satisfaction. He felt the Stoker's thick length stuffed deep inside him. His own 10-inch cock poled up from the valley where his thighs wrapped around the Stoker's muscle-narrowed waist. The penetration was complete. What was left was the "focking."

The Stoker stomped his boots, and the crowd fell back, as he carried Edward ten paces to the smooth iron cover of a throbbing engine. He eased Edward's torso down flat, pulling his rod of cock out to the neck beneath its inflated head locked inside Edward's ass-ring. They were poised against one another, with one another, in some inevitable destiny. The rhythms of *Titanic*'s mighty engines became theirs as the Stoker, slowly, then faster, began pistoning Edward's butt, driving in, drawing out, pounding in, tearing out, working together, rearing nearly apart, Edward's shouts almost as loud as the Stoker's grunts, coming harder, deeper, faster, his dick plunging to its massive root up Edward's ass, his bull-balls slam-banging into the iron engine cover.

The Stoker raised his huge arms, spread from his wide shoulders and massive hairy pecs, above his head, a triumphant victor, his hips and butt, planted firm on his booted thick legs, ramming, in rhythm to the engines, ramming his cock full-depth charge into Edward, pulling out all the way, ramming its big head again and again through the target of Edward's willing, dripping, hungry ass.

Again, they froze. They glazed over, the two of them, in the heat. The Stoker's cock was buried in Edward to the hilt. His upraised arms flexed, thick with power, the way his dick was flexing inside Edward's flexing ass.

The crowd sensed it. I knew it. The Stoker started a mighty roar. His muscular arms raised, his body fully flexed, he rammed Edward once more, held steady course deep inside him, and, fast as a flame leaps from a furnace, yanked his cock free. Posed in triumphant victory, he leaned in over Edward, laying the base pipe of his 14-inch cock topside over Edward's 10 inches.

Handless, he came.

Handless, his enormous cock shot wave upon crashing wave of white cum breaking across the shore of Edward's belly and chest and throat and face.

Handless, untouched, Edward's cock came, shooting up on the triumphant muscleman of a Stoker, hitting his hairy pectorals, creaming his belly, his rockhard, still sperming dick.

I came.

The crowd of men came.

The Stoker picked Edward up in his arms, carrying him, one forearm under Edward's knees, the other under his shoulders. His big cock, relentless, protruded hard from beneath Edward's forward buttock. Edward's own cock stood erect.

"I fock you," the Stoker said. "Now you lay the night with me."

Edward, my Edward, looked up at the Stoker, grinned, threw his arm around the giant's shoulder, and laid his cheek on the Stoker's grimy, hairy chest.

And off the Stoker carried him.

Perhaps Edward should have listened to Madame Ouspenskaya's card reading, foretelling danger, because events larger than our most fearful dreams loomed ahead, as *Titanic*, built for 24-28 knots, sped, at her captain's vanity, through the icy dark of the North Atlantic at a world-record 30 knots per hour.

Aboard *Titanic*. At sea. Westbound.
Sunday, 14 April, 1912

In the salons and smoking rooms, men toasted rumors of a record crossing. Twenty-four of *Titanic*'s 30 boilers were in service with preparations underway to light the remaining boilers for the next day's speed test. Edward was too exhausted from his night with the Stoker to accompany me to Sunday services convened in the first-class dining saloon. "Out of 2,000 passengers," Edward had gloated, "that coal-heaving Stoker chose me." Captain Smith read the service not from the *Book of Common Prayer*, but from the White Star Line's own prayer book. Shortly after 11 AM, with the ship's orchestra halfway through "O God, Our Help in Ages Past," I excused myself with a wink to the indomitable Molly Brown seated by my side. Even at service, Molly, dragged out in all her flamboyant finery, stood out like a bright yellow satin flower among the proper Astors and Vanderbilts and Ryersons attired in their subdued churchgoing blues, browns, and blacks.

"Go get 'em, sailor," she said.

I excused myself past the Thayers, the Carters, and President Taft's traveling aide Major Archibald Butt, who himself, I sensed, could hardly wait to adjourn to the fashionable *à la carte* restaurant where the George D. Wideners were to host an elegant party breakfast. Outside, near the Marconi Wireless Telegraph room, where operators Bride and Phillips were hard at work transmitting

ship's messages as well as passenger messages to inter-
mediary vessels for relay to London and New York, I met
Felix Jones, our red-headed purser who had provided so
much frolic our first night at sea. His 8-inches were bas-
keted discreetly in his tailored uniform. He grinned,
without a word, and whisked me away for a surprise he
had promised. In the wake of our leaving, Bride and
Phillips must have exchanged the knowing glances of the
straight-arrow. I heard their laughter and was not
amused.

"Some men," I said to Felix, "just don't get it."
Bride and Phillips turned back to their messages.

"To *Titanic* and eastbound ships:
Ice report in latitude 42 N, to 41.25 N,
longitude 49 W, to 50.30 W.
Saw much heavy pack ice and great number
large bergs. Also field ice.
Weather good, clear."

Waiting for me in a well-appointed, but unoccupied
second-class suite apparently reserved for discreet rendezvous, were the ship's second carpenter, Michael Brice,
and Third Officer, Samuel Maxwell, both stripped naked,
sitting in opposite Morris chairs, milking separate hard-
ons, awaiting a Sunday service of their own.

"Gentlemen," Felix said, "may I present Mr. Michael
Whitney."

Brice stood, cock jutting. Maxwell remained seated, cock rampant between his spread thighs. Felix, ever
the gentleman's gentleman, discreetly withdrew. Not
one word was spoken. Brice locked the door. I stripped.

Resonant as a deep bass drum, *Titanic*'s engines hummed beneath the light slip-slap of Max's hand spit-stroking his big 9-inch cock. He was a solid, good-looking 38, better built than most officers. His neatly trimmed beard sported a becoming streak of gray. He exuded the confidence of a man whose logged nautical miles combined would have taken him around the world a hundred times. Brice had shipped out with him more than once. They had an understanding. Their relationship was pure lust. They rarely spoke. Their common interest, on long trans-Atlantic crossings, no more than the sexual gymnastics they staged together.

They liked to facefuck.

Double facefuck.

Cock to cock.

Both their dicks sliding together down one throat.

The rugged carpenter Brice and the commanding officer Max. Brice, blond and thick. Max, dark and regal. Brice, of almost equal age, 34 or so, both of them older men than I at 22. Brice with 9 inches moved toward me. My own 8 inches rose like a hard knot. Brice's tool-hardened hand clamped my shoulder, guiding me like a good boy down on my knees.

When my knees fold, my mouth opens. Some men like that in a man.

Brice did. He was no talk, all moves. He spit into the palm of his hand and spit-shined the big head of his cock, stalking on his big legs toward me, his fat prick aimed for docking in the open port of my waiting mouth. His coarsened carpenter's hand had calloused his carpenter's cockhead. Its pink skin, worn rough, felt like the smoothest of fine sandpaper in my mouth. If ever a man were meant to "polish my sharp tongue down a notch," as my father had said when he shipped me off to Oxford, it was not my British tutors, it was Brice.

He worked my sucking lips and probed my mouth, driving left and right, tunneling for maximum headroom, surveying with his rod the drop he'd clicked down into my lower jaw, like a miner opening a cave wide enough for heavy machinery, to fit his cock inside up tight against Max's dick. Max! Who liked to deep-six his long, lean shaft down voyager's throats while Brice alternately plugged left cheek, right cheek, waltzing matilda, one, two, three.

A pair of lip-rippers they were, but my cock was up for the stretch even if my mouth had doubts. If Edward had taken the Stoker's 14 inches up his ass, my mouth could swallow the 18-inch double facefuck I saw coming. If not, by the time we docked in New York, I'd regret forever falling short of my lover's titanic feat.

I sucked a mouthful of Brice's globular head, wrapping my lips tight around the underlip of the corona. I felt I was swallowing one of Mr. Edison's electric bulbs: hot, large, and hard. I moaned. Behind the head of his slow-probing prow, my eyes, almost crossed, looked down the veined length of his sturdy, studhorse cock. He drove me over half-backwards. My hands left my cock to support me from behind. My head tilted up flat as a plate. His cock angled like a lever forging open my lips a crack, a crack wide enough for Max, moving slowly, cruising into view over my forehead, cock first, with a crystal glass in his hand.

He poured at least three fingers of absinthe over the hot head of Brice's cock, three fingers of 68% alcohol that

I gulped without resistance down my throat. They knew what they were doing. My teeth retracted. My jaw dropped. My throat opened to a tunnel of fire. My head went absent without leave, absinthe without leave, I say now, and I fell into my sexual essence: I was no less than an open mouth with a hard cock kneeling before 18 inches of dick backed with enough male authority to rouse me to a fevered, perverted pitch, hungry, starving for the facefuck of the seedbearers, who, dickhead to dickhead, came v-shaped from left and right to rape my willing mouth.

Edward once had worked his sculler's fist all the way into my mouth and my passion for him had let me take the pleasure of his hard-knuckled fullness, my teeth wrapped tight around his thick wrist. My shipboard lust was no less for this anonymous pair of silent, brooding, insistent seamen. I was no more than a nine-hour virgin, having shot my load the night before watching the Stoker fuck Edward, but that was five hours more than I needed to reload fully, especially fueled by the sight of their big bodies, pronged with their pair of absinthe-slick dicks, closing in on me.

All the giddiness of Edward dubbing me "Queen Michael" and Molly crowning me with her embarrassing Hapsburg tiara was forgotten in the serious business at hand.

I had cock to suck.

I thought.

But I was wrong.

Brice and Max weren't seeking sucking.

They were fuckers, face-fuckers.

I was their face.

I was incidental.

Their unspoken-lovers' game was feeling their two dicks rubbing together, slip-sliding in and out, each revolving around the other, the way two athletic men clasp sweaty gladiatorial hands, gripping fists, intensely face to face, in the kind of pub arm-wrestling so popular throughout Britain, so scorned at Cambridge, so practiced at Oxford—arm wrestling introduced by the Romans centuries before. Never had I wanted to be a stranger in the world. Edward loved my American sense of exploration, and Brice and Max were new territory I took to with no map but my hard cock.

The two seamen got a high-speed, top-knot run for their money. I was every inch as much a cocksucker as they were face-fuckers. Edward had said he loved me because I was never passive, always active, even with his 10-inch oar rowing my deep ass. Brice and Max got the same treatment. I clicked my jaw down another notch and suctioned both their cocks into my mouth, holding them both hardon in my stuffed cheeks. They fucked together. Their side-by-side dicks alternately chugged my cheeks. Two man-size cocks, shipmates, buddies, silent lovers never speaking their own names, dick-to-dick, shaft-sliding slick, neck and neck, their matched 9-inch naval "short arms," fisted at the top with almost twin heads, wrestling cock-to-cock for advantage in the fighting arena of my mouth. What a bout! What a scrap!

My mouth felt like a writhing snake pit inside a boxer's punching bag.

In tandem, they slow-jabbed my face, Brice pummeling my cheeks, Max driving deeper, outdistancing Brice, his cockhead jamming the back of my mouth, stretching open the O-ring to my throat, pulling back behind Brice, taking my left cheek away from him, forcing him to my right cheek, their rods crossed like duellists' swords across my flat tongue, Brice fighting back, both cocks, competing, head next to head, stuffing my left cheek, ramming together, foaming my salivating mouth with their dripping cock slits, the licorice-sweet absinthe running deep fire down my throat, hungry for the depthplunge, eager for the cheek joust, lusting for their combined 18 inches working my face, half expecting their cockheads to ram through the smooth plate of both my cheeks, crisscrossed cocks, smooth cheeks, gaping mouth, startled eyes.

That image of penis-rampant clicked in the back of my head as the perfect family crest my straightlaced Boston Brahmin father deserved! The face of his wide-eyed, wide-mouthed son, with 18 inches of cock jutting triumphant from his cheeks, mounted on the mansion trophy wall like some strange-horned mythical beast hunted and killed by ancient ancestors. What a jape on my father who had never in his life even spoken the word *penis*!

A thought is but an instant in sex. Perhaps fantasy triggered by hardon reality is all of sex. The truth is the double entry of Brice and Max was the calm before the storm. Their cocks, colliding with my cheeks, forged hot in their foreplay. Together, they pulled out, popping my lips, my jaw hanging open, my tongue drooling ropes of absinthe spit to the twin heads of their dicks. Brice grabbed my hair to hold my head steady. Max delicately drove two fingers up my nostrils, tilting my head into place. My mouth, gasping for breath, hung like an open and willing target already on fire, burning like a boiler

stoked by their sex-shovels. The three of us hung poised
and ready. Brice spit down on his sandpaper dickhead
and rammed me first, churning up my cheeks, his hand
gripping my hair, Max's fingers stuffing my nose. I was
foaming like a mad dog in the noonday sun, loving it,
knowing who I was, not knowing what I was, my mind
reeling mixed metaphors my professors would have
shamed me for, but here was no shame, not in this sport-
ing frolic. *Titanic* was a dreamship come true, a phan-
tasm of imagination made so real only a fool could not
actualize realities larger than his wildest fantasies.

Max tilted my nose left and right. Brice plunged
right and left, calling for more absinthe. Max poured the
hot liqueur straight from the bottle on Brice's cock. I
gulped the churning foam, sinking beneath the battering ram of cock. Max pulled my nose up, gently. My eyes
opened wide. The length of his huge dick spanned across
my face, forehead to chin, its head red, slick, and dripping. Blue veins, thick as snakes, coiled tight around the
log of his thick shaft. Brice held steady, docked in my
right cheek. Max's face grinned way above his cock which
loomed larger, closer than his head. He held my nose in
place. Quiet settled on the three of us frozen in place like
competing athletes waiting for the starter's gun. Sure as
shooting, Max, driving his hard ramrod, pumping it in
slow tattoo against my face, teased open my lips locked
down on Brice's cock, slipping down alongside the length
of carpenter cock, never hesitating, his cockhead, driv-
en by his shaft, sliding across my tongue, snaking inch
by inch to the back of my throat, docking with the O-ring,
touching, teasing the membrane, readying to screw my
head on to my shoulders.

He pulled his fingers slowly from my nostrils as he slowly drove his cock down my throat. He gave my breath back and took it away. Nose then mouth. Controlled breathing. Perfect moves. What could have been barbaric was athletic, even dancelike. I wanted Max and Brice. On their terms. They had won me over, conquered me. They stuffed my mouth and throat with too much cock for me to suck. My face was an open hole, a berth, home port, safe harbor. We were in delicate waters. I surrendered to their double-fuck.

Max slithered down my gullet, inching down, inching out, then down again, his fullness each time gaining deeper purchase on my throat, impaling me with hard cock, Brice, slow-pumping my cheeks, twin engines, working up full steam, easing me new into their accustomed fuck, timing themselves, jab, slip, slide, dip, ram, building the volume of cock, building the pace of fuck, slick they were, slicking themselves into me, chugging up their pace, throttling their alternating pistoning moves, their hard cocks stiffening harder side by side, two dick-buddies, fucking one face.

I've never yet met a man who, falling to his knees, did not wish his best friends could see him at that moment, some gasping in shocked horror, some applauding in envy. Going down is always the best revenge. On everyone. Even God.

Together they weighed more than a solid-built 300 pounds of force, irresistible, driving their tag-team cocks into my mouth. Max was rooted *basso profundo* deep in my throat strumming chords on my vocal cords. Brice took the treble clef jamming my cheeks *staccato*. Would that Edward had seen the operatic spectacle of our trio swaying in gathered fuck rhythm, building toward horned climax. Brice grunted more than Max and Brice's grunts directed the pace of their duet. His cock was swelling larger in my mouth, pulsing, throbbing alongside Max's iron rod. Cock-taste is like no other taste: sweaty, salty, sweet, and dirty. We fucked in perfect, rugged harmony. Upstairs, the band played on. Downstairs, the pair of seamen, carpenter and captain, force-fed their matched cocks. Brice was first to pass his limit: his fuck-speed picked up 10 knots, his grunts grew lower, tenser, his cock a battering gun pummeling my cheeks.

Max was not far behind. He put one muscular arm around Brice's broad shoulders and pulled him in close, poising him for the strike, ramming Brice's cock as much into his own hard shaft as into my cheeks. With a roar, Brice reared his head back, then whipped his face forward, staring down at the sight of his pumping cock double-fucking my face. He shot hard bullets of hot clot, filling my cheeks, ramming me, sliding alongside Max, his massive cock driving past his explosions, cocks colliding, driving Max deeper, the taste and smell of his seed boiling down my throat alongside Max's descending, pumping rod.

Max himself began a low groan in his big nuts. My throat opened and, rebellious fallen angel that I am, I swallowed him in deeper, taking half the head of Brice's dick along. Max twisted, stared hard down at my face, and, to reward me or discipline me, I have never known, drove his cock, shaft-fast past Brice's cock, and buried himself deep down, Brice holding my head by my hair. Max, profane as a parrot, cursed like a sailor, ramming his pulsing dick in place, shooting his depth-charge of white fluming sperm, exploding hot snot in my guts, down my throat, up out my nose, huge tidal waves of their mixed cum flooding from my lips, their two dicks, twisting hard, fighting for space, me choking, them panting, their big stiff pricks, held tight in place, forcing me to swallow, their fingers re-feeding me the cum escaping my lips, their draining dicks slowly, ever so slowly softening down to two fat snakes nesting in my mouth, licking them, sucking up their cum, them suctioning their twin 9-inchers from my face. When they saw I had cum without touching myself, they laughed, pulled me to my feet, and dropped me gently to the carpet. *Titanic* hummed along the full length of my backside as we sped together, fuck buddies, across the North Atlantic.

Edward thought my "Sunday picnic" was "ever so jolly." He said, "I rendezvous again with the Stoker. Tonight at 10. He wants to lock me in a cell in the brig, break in, and take me by force."

"Be careful," I said. "Remember Madame Ouspenskaya's Tarot reading."

"Don't be ridiculous," Edward said. "She's no mystic. She's no more than a nanny babysitting that Egyptian mummy Lord Ashcroft is sending to the New York Museum."

"That *cursed* Egyptian mummy," I said.

"Poo," Molly said at supper. "Of course, the mummy's cursed. No one pays admission if there's no curse. That's the thrill."

"That's one kind of thrill," I said.

Edward winked at Molly and they laughed uproariously.

John Jacob Astor stared straight ahead.

At 9:30 exactly, Edward looked at his gold pocket watch, and excused himself from Molly and me, and our jolly party, in the Main Salon. Edward whispered, "He said he'd lock me up and throw away the key!"

At 10 exactly, stripped naked, his 10 inches hard in front of him, Edward found himself kneeling, locked in a cell, sucking the muscular Stoker's massive 14-inch cock through the steel bars. At 10:30, Edward, jacking his own cock, was ordered by the Stoker to back down and lie on the floor of the cell. The Stoker, as lead coal-man, left to check on his boiler crew. Edward, disobe-diently, aristocratically, abandoning the common seaman's order to lie on the cold floor, lay alone on the single bunk in the cell, his cock in his hand, a smile on his face.

"I'm chilly," Molly said.

"I am always chilled," Madame Ouspenskaya stated.

Our table laughed. Even Mrs. J. J. Astor.

"Indeed," said the famous mystery writer Jacques Futrelle, who six days previous had celebrated his 37th birthday at a fashionable London restaurant. "An Amer-ican gentleman told my wife that Captain Maxwell told him that between 7 and 10 PM the air temperature has dropped from 43 to 32 degrees."

"The promenade deck," Mrs. Futrelle said, "was noticeably cool this afternoon."

"Still," Madame Ouspenskaya said, "the sea is calm."

"There is no moon," Molly said wistfully.

"But the stars," I said, "shine brightly."

"Not as brightly as my diamond Hapsburg tiara,"

Molly said. She leaned her bosom close to me. "I hope you've stored it safely in the ship's vault."

"Actually," I said, "it's in our suite."

"You're as careless as me," she said. "No wonder I like you."

At 11:40, half our table looked up. The other half kept laughing, talking animatedly above the lustrous eight-man orchestra directed by bandmaster Hartley.

"What was that?" Molly asked.

"It sounded," Madame Ouspenskaya intoned, "as if a finger were drawn against the side of the ship."

The look on her face made my temperature drop faster than the evening air. At 21 knots, *Titanic* sped through the water at 300 feet in less than 10 seconds. "It has to be nothing," I said. "Look. Nothing has changed. The dancers. The music. The ballroom."

Molly agreed. "You fellas and gals should feel the earthquakes in Colorado."

In the Grand Ballroom there was absolutely no sense of shock. Below decks, deep inside the ship, in Boiler Room 6, on the starboard side, the Stoker heard the impact's crunching, and then a sound like thunder rolling toward him. A line of water was pouring through a thin gash in the ship's side two feet above the stoke-hole floor. He ordered his coal gang fast up the boiler room's emergency ladder.

Edward, pounding his pud, locked solitary two decks above in the brig cell, felt nothing but the shuddering of his own passion.

Below decks, watertight doors slammed closed amid the raucous shrill of the alarm bells activated by First Officer William Murdock on the bridge.

In the postal sorting room on G Deck, the clerks began their hasty removal of mail to the higher decks. The elevators were not working, but the lights remained on without a flicker.

"Assess the damage," Captain Edward Smith ordered. To his dismay, at midnight, as Sunday, 14 April, became Monday, 15 April, he found that no more than twelve square feet of *Titanic* had been breached, but those twelve feet stretched, in a tear 3 inches wide, 300 feet along the ship's length, flooding five compartments. The ship could float with even the first four compartments flooded; but she could not survive the breaching of the fifth. "Had we but a moon," the Captain said, "we might have seen the face of the berg." Well he might have said, "Had we but a moon, we might have seen the face of God."

At 12:15, the Marconi Wireless room sent *Titanic*'s first distress signals. Twenty-one-year-old Robert Hallam, wireless operator on the eastbound *Carpathia*, 58 miles south of *Titanic*'s position, was stripping for bed, sleepily touching his penis, and about to turn off his receiver for the night, when he caught the call. *Carpathia*'s Captain wheeled his course around making his slow, careful way through the ice fields of the open sea.

"I believe we've stopped," I said.

Still nothing changed. Through the Grand Ballroom window, I could see into the first-class dining rooms. Stewards were putting the finishing touches on the breakfast table settings.

Molly kicked one high-buttoned shoe up on the white linen table cloth. "My feet are still dry!" She made everyone laugh, but our laughter, our laughter—that had changed.

By 12:30, Thayers, Astors, Wideners, Ryersons, husbands, wives, families, accustomed to giving orders, not taking them, assembled on A Deck's forward side. The band stood on deck playing popular songs from operetta and the musical stage, and even the new sensation, ragtime.

I was frantic to find Edward.

Titanic was built to accommodate 2,435 passengers and 860 crew, a total of 3,295. On her maiden voyage, she carried 2,228 with 14 lifeboats and collapsibles; capacity: 980. At first, the boats were half-full, occupants boarding reluctantly, as much ashamed of doubting *Titanic*'s vaunted unsinkable reputation as they were afraid of the cold open sea at night. Exploding distress flairs rocketed like fireworks through the night sky. Near panic ensued.

"Women and children first!"

"It was a woman," I said, "who thought up that line."

"Women," Molly Brown said, "have always outsmarted men."

Portside, the more crowded side, only females and children were allowed in the boats by the crew armed with guns. Starboard, men could board if no women were present. Had we stupid cattle known then what we knew only later!

I saw no coalmen from below decks. If anyone could bring my Edward back up safe, it was the Stoker.

When 13-year-old heir Jack Ryerson was prevented by the loading officer from accompanying his mother, millionaire John Jacob Astor placed a woman's hat on the young man's head and pronouced, "So, now, you're a girl and you may go."

Molly's eyes lit up.

"I must find Edward," I said.

"Edward," Molly said, "knows how to take care of himself."

"This is a charade," I said. "None of us knows how to take care of ourselves."

Molly tossed me a look. "I oughta slap you," she said. She dragged me up the slanting A Deck to her suite, ripping open her closet, throwing gown upon gown on the bed.

"I can't," I said. "I've never worn women's clothes in my life and I certainly won't now."

"Don't be an ass."

"I can't."

"Join the charade," she said.

It was 1:48 AM by the clock on Molly's *escritoire*. She threw a red ballgown over me. "Why red?" I said.

"Because men always want to save a scarlet woman!" She plopped a heavy fur coat across my shoulders, turned up the collar, buttoned it at my throat, so recently occupied by Brice and Max, and plopped the broadest brimmed hat she could find on my head.

"This is cowardly, you know," I said.

"This," she corrected me, "is survival. You and your kind should understand that."

Me and my kind. How often had I heard that. But my kind had narrowed down to Edward, God knew where, locked down in the hold of the ship. "I don't care about my kind."

"I care about your kind," Molly said. She kissed me almost tenderly. "Come on, Queen Michael! Follow me! As far as I can tell, it's every man for himself, and hell will take the hindmost!"

Truly, I didn't want to die by drowning or freezing in the dark cold waters of the North Atlantic. I understood the code of old-style manners followed gamely by the rich gentlemen standing serenely on the decks, waving to their wives, lying in their teeth, assuring them they'd follow in the next lifeboats. In my red ballgown, I rode on Molly's arm with my moustache buried in her fur collar. I spied among the elegant men, searching for Edward.

On A Deck, Madeleine Astor's dog, Kitty, ran barking back and forth. From C Deck, the immigrant crowds in steerage raced up the stairs to first class, only to be trapped below stairs by the locked iron gates. *Titanic* was sinking fast into the water. The decks tilted sharply. The electric lights burned brightly. The band played. Flares hissed, flared, and burst overhead. Crystal goblets and flutes and bowls slid from the tables. The tables slid across the floors. Heavy machinery below was booming, breaking loose, sliding backwards toward the bow, pulling us down faster under its weight.

I noticed Molly carried an extra dress and coat and hat. "Do you intend to change?" I asked, overcome with the sarcasm of gallows humor. "Into something smart for a sinking?"

"It's for Edward."

"We must find him." My heart raced. My head spun. My humor changed. Everyone at that moment was leaving someone. Women, men, children. Separated. The seriousness of the situation made us all quiet for a moment, internal, listening to the cries of fate.

"We'll find him," Molly said.

Suddenly, the wild crowd pushed and shoved around us pressing us closer to portside Lifeboat 6 which was already descending over the side. In an instant, strong arms lifted me up into the air. It was Brice. "Come on, lady, here you go!"

"Brice," I said. "It's me."

"You!" He almost dropped me.

"Jump with me, Brice."

"It's my duty to stay."

"Fuck your duty. Save your life."

"I'm crew," he said solemnly. "You're a passenger."

"Don't be stupid."

He smiled ruefully. "Promise me one thing." He pulled me close to him.

"Anything."

Edward was not to be seen over Brice's shoulder.

"Live for me."

"Don't be British, Brice."

Disaster was upon us all.

"Live your life!"

Time slowed to a halt. Everything became deliberate, meaningful, absurd.

Brice smiled and said quite calmly, as if we were standing in a pub, "In New York. A new Turkish Bath. Run by the Police and Firemen Benevolent Association."

"Brice, we're sinking!"

"Go there!"

"Climb into this boat, and I won't have to make a donation in your memory."

"Rather!" He grinned like a sailor always expecting this inevitable moment.

"What's the place called?"

"The Everhard," he said.

Before I could say, "I must find Edward," Brice dropped me five feet over the side into the descending lifeboat. Molly, tossed over by Officer "Max" Maxwell, landed on top of me, all but crushing me, save for the drag she'd hauled along for Edward.

"Just shut up," she whispered.

Brice and Max stood together in the melee on the crowded deck. Over us all, a flare hissed up into the dark night and exploded.

Molly rose up and she shouted, making good use of her music hall voice, demanding another sailor. Just like Molly. Just like me. Demanding another sailor. "Throw me a sailor!" she bellowed. "I need a man to help row this boat full of sobbin' women." She turned to me and whispered again. "You see? You'll be more help here rowing in a woman's dress than standing in your pants on deck singing hymns."

Brice tossed a sailor twelve feet down into our descending boat. It was Felix Jones. "I'm not a common sailor," Felix announced to everyone. "I'm a purser." I pulled my collar up and my hat brim down. "G'wan," Felix whispered. "I'd know you anywhere. We both can thank Mr. Brice and Officer Max and consider ourselves lucky."

As soon as we hit the water, Molly stood in the prow of the boat, like Washington crossing the Delaware, barking orders, commanding Felix and me and the 24 women in the boat to row for our lives. At that moment, the unsinkable Molly Brown became fixed in history and legend. I rowed with all my might, tears streaming down my face for my Edward, surely lost below decks.

It was a night so clear we could see stars reflecting

themselves on a sea smooth as a mirror. The noise of the ship was enormous. People wailing, jumping, screaming in the night. Flare guns. Pistol shots. Random music, *nearer*, singing, *my God*, praying, *to thee*. Then like thunder, *Titanic* split in two. The bow sank almost instantly. There was a moment of almost absolute silence. It was 2:15 AM. Then thunder again. *Titanic*'s stern reared high in the water, bright, brilliant with light, phallic, magnificent in disaster, tall as a skyscraper. In a crashing avalanche, everything movable on the ship slid violently into the water. The postal clerks, dedicated to faithful delivery of their mail, were swept downwards in a tidal wave of envelopes and parcels. Hundreds and hundreds of people, a thousand, shouting, more than a thousand, screaming, were thrown into the cold sea thrashing in the 28 degree water. At 2:18 the lights in *Titanic*'s stern flickered and failed. *Titanic* stood vertically for ninety seconds, and at 2:20, the stern of the great ship slipped gurgling beneath the surface of the sea, sending up one immense white burst of steam toward the unblinking stars.

Two thousand people watched *Titanic* sink; 706 were in lifeboats.

Less than a mile away, an iceberg floated slowly on the current, a scrap of red and black paint smeared like whore's lipstick along its face.

Madame Ouspenskaya, too old to row, sat regally in the bow of Lifeboat 6, fully opposite Molly. Her face was impassive. Voices, passengers floating, swimming, freezing, sinking in the sea, cried out for help in the night.

I strained to hear, really not to hear, Edward's voice.

"Don't listen," Felix said. "They'd only swamp us."

Against their distant fading cries, our lifeboat lapped quietly on the ink-cold sea.

Molly wrapped the clothes meant for Edward around Mr. Astor's five-months-pregnant wife.

We rowed in the starry dark in silence. Other lifeboats floated on the quiet waters.

"Edward will be in one of the other boats," Molly said.

At 4:10, less than two hours after *Titanic*'s sinking, *Carpathia* loaded the first of the survivors up from the sea. Dawn and *Titanic* both lay eastwards behind us. *Carpathia*'s passengers, standing at first in awed silence, lined the rails as we were hoisted aboard in slings and bosuns' chairs. They cried for us. They pointed their fingers, and held their hands to their mouths, and lamented the boats, carrying only 5 or 25, designed for 40.

"You see," Maggie said, stripping her ballgown from me in the privacy of a stateroom. "You took no one's place."

Second Officer Charles H. Lightoller was the last survivor hoisted from the sea by creaking pulley to the deck of *Carpathia*. In all, only 706 souls of *Titanic*'s 2,228 passengers and crew survived the sinking.

1,522 died.

Including Edward Wedding.

My love. My lover.

Asleep in the deep, hopefully held in the strong arms of the Stoker.

The world was stunned. The only land station, immediately after the sinking of *Titanic*, powerful enough to receive the *Carpathia*'s messages sat atop Wanamaker's Department Store in Manhattan, where its 21-year-old operator, David Sarnoff, who was soon to found CBS, scribbled the garbled names of the survivors for release to the press.

On *Carpathia*'s return to New York, more than 10,000 people gathered on the Battery, at Manhattan's southern tip, as we passed, docking at 8:30 PM, at pier 54, at the foot of West 14th Street, where photographers' magnesium flares exploded like rockets in the dark of the spring night, and the silent movie cameras rolled.

Two days later, John Jacob Astor, millionaire, body number 124, was found in the sea, wearing men's clothes: a blue serge suit, a handkerchief monogrammed *JJA*, a brown flannel shirt, and brown boots with red rubber soles.

A Tale of Gay Marriage...

BRIDESHEAD OF FRANKENSTEIN REVISITED

Sebastian, that certain summer, I found intolerable, scooping up uncut rentboys with a net along the nude beach on the Bavarian strand. The young men liked Sebastian's naturally muscular body as much as his decadent blond good looks, and his dollars *Americain*. We, Sebastian and I, were in a slow drag becoming undestined as lovers. "It's still the same old story...as time goes by." We were "Skinners." Our foreskins had brought us together, but the handwriting was on the wall. Strange smegma was on the sheets.

For myself, I preferred the company of Anne Rice's *Beauty Trilogy* as well as that of the minister's handsome son, an overheated and under-ventilated classic blond boy of 18 who relieved his sexual tension through meditation and intense gymnastics. We had met, Dieter and I, eyes first, across the small tables of an outdoor cafe. Something in the breeze, perhaps the sweet smell wafting from the cheese inside his blond foreskin, or was it his dazzle in the noon light, caused me to raise my glance from *Beauty*'s frolics.

The sea, wind, and blue sky combined into a sudden explosion of sunburst blondness. His hair raised in the gust of breeze and fell perfectly back in place. Very *Deco*! He smiled and dropped his hand from his sweating glass of Perrier down to his naked thigh. He smiled again. I set my marker in *Beauty* and smiled back. He knew I was the companion of the infamous Sebastian and that knowledge made him, if not bold, then daring.

Sebastian at last was good for something.

Dieter moved his hand up his thigh, rubbing it across his white nylon athletic shorts, dropping the concave palm of his strong gymnast hands over the big convex cup of his cock and balls, groping himself, adroitly, for just a moment. He pulled the nylon shorts so tight I could see the transparent outline of his cock.

He was uncut.

Even his face was the confident face of an uncut male.

I'd spied not just the size of his dick, but a clear outline of his large nipple of foreskin wrinkled, folded, and long as a sausage sleeve tied off with two inches to spare.

My own nine-inch cock hardened. I shivered with uncontrollable pleasure as my cockhead mushroomed out through my tight foreskin that rolled back and down my shaft like an O-ring on a sky-bound Shuttle. Tight 'skin. I like it. I got it. I wondered about the minister's son. How tight is the foreskin of a cherub?

I sipped the last of my Bavarian coffee.

Oh God. Ohgodogodogod!

A bead of sweat, bright as a crystal, formed in the cleft of his strong blond chin, caught the sun, glistened and dropped to the top of the channel between his lean hard pecs. The tip of my tongue grew dry and hard. I could tell he appreciated the subtle sensuality as the sweat-bead, slower than slow motion, micrometered down his chest, stopping for an even instant in a direct horizontal line between his sweet brown tits, themselves small and sculpted and aching with virgin hunger.

His chest and tensely lean torso were not hairy, yet he was not smooth. His pecs, belly, forearms, and legs were downed with the babiest of blond hair, enough to catch the sun, adding to his physique an aura of gold. He was an angel skimming the ground. He sat motionless. My cock strained hard in my shorts. My foreskin felt tight as a rubber band around my shaft. I sucked in the smell of my smegma packed in under the corona of my cock.

I wanted him, with my hands gripped tight in his blond hair, to teethe the cheese from my cock.

I wanted him. I wanted to suckle on his foreskin, sipping its hidden juices and clots of blond *fromage*.

He drew a breath. On purpose, he drew a breath, dislodging from between his pecs, the bead of sweat that slowly rolled down the maze-way of his gymnast-carved abs, not straight down, but following the hard-flexed muscle groups, left, then right, like a silver pinball. I imagined buttons on his slender hips that flipped flippers. I wanted to shoot the bead of sweat back up his torso, hitting his nipples, scoring points, lights flashing, bells dinging, with the same concentrated intensity a champion pinballer passionately keeps his silver ball in play.

I must have looked like a fool standing on my own tongue. When the sweat bead reached his navel, it dropped in, stopped, stayed. He smiled and flexed his washboard belly popping the bead up and free, rolling down toward the band of his shorts. I dreaded its absorption into the white nylon.

He was even better than I thought. At the last possible moment, as the sweat rolled to his waist, he pulled his hand from his crotch. He fingered into the waistband and triangled it opened and the sweat bead ran down, disappearing into the almost visible blond bush growing around his big jock cock. He flipped his finger, snapping the waistband closed like a slingshot, and for the first time, he opened his mouth and laughed the deep laugh that comes from loaded stud teenage bullballs.

I will never love anyone as much as I loved him that moment. If my whole life ever flashes before my eyes, I hope the film gets stuck on that one frame: where the blond muscular boy laughed as the bead of hot sweat ran down the length of his ten-inch cock. He had everything. Even *that*: a big dick. Blond. Blue-eyed. Built. Sweet-natured. Innocent. And a ten-inch cock. Two inches more than Sebastian, I might add, and one inch more than me.

Was I in luck, in love, or what?

There is only one sin in life. When a Bavarian Methodist minister's muscular son invites you to suck his big blond uncut ten-inch cock, and you will not do it. Me? I'm no sinner. "This could be heaven," the Eagles sang on *Hotel California*, "this could be hell." I was going down on that boy. I was going to swallow him till his foreskin came out my asshole.

With all due respect to the genius of Anne Rice, I dropped her *Beauty* for his. He was the perfect blond youth who sang "Tomorrow Belongs to Me" in *Cabaret*.

He was the lean-muscled ideal Dr. Frankenfurter sang about in *Rocky Horror Picture Show*: "In just seven days, I'll make you a man!" He was the perfect, sculpted blond the Marines put on recruiting posters.

And he hadn't been around the block. He had an innocence. He was not one of the village boys who worked the beaches and hotels where the likes of Thomas Mann and Tennessee Williams once spoiled them with too much of everything, making them mercenary, hard, and liars. I was tired of rough-trade German and Bavarian boys force-feeding me the cheese pastry from their thick European foreskins.

I wanted the minister's tasty son.

I wanted his fresh innocence.

I wanted his innocence to give rebirth to mine.

The only hitch was Sebastian. He wanted whatever I wanted more than he wanted what he wanted. Ever since that bed-and-breakfast night we spent in a freezing castle in Transylvania, Sebastian had turned into the bride of Frankenstein. You know how some gay guys are; they latch onto a schtick and can't let go, repeating the same act or the same catch phrase like "See how you are" or, worse, "Thank you," a million times a day as an answer to no matter what you say.

Just so Sebastian. He was a film queen. He'd forced me through a truly gross week at the Cannes Film Festival. I saw more films than I wanted to, and Sebastian saw none. He spent the week cruising like a human mattress up and down the sand, *Gauloises* in one hand, champagne bottle in the other. No matter what happened to us, or who we were with, or what was the conversation, he continuously spouted *non-sequiturs*: "Just like

Susan Hayward in *I Want to Live*," or, "How Bette Davis!"

"Transylvania" was his latest affectation. Why he identified with Elsa Lanchester, the female monster, and not with the male, puzzled me. Sebastian was masculine enough. At least on the outside. Through the chatty haze of his martinis, he thought he was terribly clever as, without realizing it, he was driving me farther away. Our summer tour had been meant to bring us closer together. It took Transylvania to make me realize I hated Sebastian.

"You and this preacher's kid haven't a chance. You're just Sandra Dee in *A Summer Place*. And he's Troy Donahue and I want his foreskin." He sipped his 1000th martini. "We agreed what was mine was yours and what was yours was mine."

"Here's a new word, Sebastian. *Disagreement*."

"You so piss me off.

"You're so easy to piss off. You're a queen."

"You're a cocksucker."

"Better a cocksucker than a queen. When I get up off my knees, you're still a queen."

That didn't end the argument, but it ended the conversation.

"Here's your hat," he said. "Don't let the door hit you when you leave."

"So long. Farewell. Auf Wiedersehen," I said.

"I don't need to be Barbra in *On a Clear Day* to know where you're going."

I sped our rented Peugeot through the village streets, heading to Dieter's house, the parsonage and school, where he lived with his mother and father and three younger brothers, whose coming of age I knew,

would make returning to this village every summer for
the next six years, a delight.

I drove, remembering that first day at the outdoor
cafe, how it had happened, how Dieter had stood up at
his table and stretched his full body in the blinding sun.
His dick and balls hung transparent in his white nylon
running shorts. He was hard. He winked at me. I rose
from my chair, forgetting *Beauty* on the table, and walked
toward him. His beauty grew with each step nearer. My
stiff cock made me drag my leg.

He put out his hand to me. I took it. His gymnast
palm was cool and hard from working the parallel bars.
His grip was firm. Not rough. Not soft. Just right. He
smelled the sweet smell of young men who have not yet
begun the long menu of grown-up poisons and addictions.

He smelled, his strongest smell, after the first
sweaty waft from his hairy blond armpits, of smegma.
He held my hand long after the handshake ended, and
then, right there in front of God and everybody, he placed
my hand on his hard cock, guiding my fingers to his two-
inch foreskin on his ten-inch cock, stretching it between
my thumb and index finger.

"It's all yours," he said.

Back in Kansas City, we always laughed about the
"PK's," the Preacher's Kids who were wilder than any-
body else in town. I was about to find the same thing in
Zeider bei der See, Bavaria.

He led me from the cafe to the ancient stone gym-
nasium, built in the 14th century, with his father's
present high-vaulted church set upon its foundation at
the turn of this century. Fantasy and charm.

"No one uses it anymore. Just me. And, sometimes,

my brothers."

He smiled making me imagine him taking his younger brothers one by one to the cellar gym for a work-out on the rings and the parallel bars, naked, always nude, their growing young dicks flopping on turns and tumbles, all four brothers with matching thick foreskins they'd strip back after their workouts, exhausted, to let the sweaty heads of their cocks breathe, laughing, dipping their fingers into their foreskins and feeding each other their steaming headcheese like chip dip. Once he had tied together all four 'skins, his and his three brothers, wrapping them with rawhide and making them play tug-of-war. "So they will grow up to be men," he said, "tough as their foreskins."

Uncut!

Uncut!

Uncut!

The way Sebastian wanted the uncut versions of movies, I wanted the uncut version of males. That's why he was a bride, and I was a groom, born to groom uncut dick, groom uncut horse dick.

Some men are lucky enough to know that their destiny, their purpose in living, lies hidden in the tight foreskins of young men.

I know me. Dieter recognized me. He saw my face. His foreskin twitched. He knew me for the true-blue "Skinner" I was.

"We are brothers," he said, "under the 'skin."

No shit, Sherlock!

I drove the Peugeot quietly up the drive heading to the back of the church where I knew the door to the gym would be unlatched and he would be waiting for me, sweaty from his workout, his hungry uncut cock arching up, wanting service.

He stood naked under a single light next to the parallel bars. He said nothing. His eyes spoke all. I moved closer. He turned, placed his chalked hands and taped wrists on the shoulder-high wooden bars, and, without so much as the tiniest jump from his feet, lifted his whole body using only his arms.

The movement tightened the definition of his muscles.

He was hard as a rock and he was rock hard.

He held his position. I knew mine. I crawled between the bars and knelt below him, my face a foot under his Thuringer cock which stood out and up 45-degrees above the horizontal. He did not move. I leaned forward and sucked his toes, first one, then all of them, licking the salt-sweet soles of his feet and tonguing his hard heels. His strength was amazing.

I leaned up and opened my mouth, wanting his foreskin-cock reigning above me. He began to do slow dips, lowering his shoulders down almost to where his hands gripped the bars. He raised his legs at the knee behind him and crossed his feet. Each dip brushed the tip of his 'skin across my face, going down, going up. He lavished me with his tube of 'skin, teasing me.

"Give me your innocence," I begged.

He laughed, as well he should have. "Then I give you my cock." He dropped slowly to the floor. "Suck my foreskin."

I pulled the two-inch tube to my nose and breathed in its heady aroma. I stretched the 'skin open and fit it tube-tight around my nose, snorkeling deep inside the clean, cheesy darkness, snorting like a pig for truffles of smegma. Big young meat always tops itself with clots of melting cheese. His aroma was so sweet and strong, I almost hyper-ventilated.

"You will eat it now," he said. His voice was sweet but commanding. So German.

I let go of his foreskin. It closed down tight. Its iris-eye stared me straight in the face. Its folds wrapped in soft flesh rings around the huge head of his hidden cock. A long strand of clear gleat drooled from the iris. He took hold of the 'skin and stretched the two inches to three, then four.

"It is big, ja? Bigger than you imagined? I have trained it. I have disciplined it."

He put his beautiful hands on his long, thick shaft, and stripped the foreskin back, slow, slow, so slow, slow as the most expert Skinner. The big lip suctioned back down over his mushroom cockhead. Its rosy blond crown shined with 'skin juice. His smell was clean, dirty, athletic, angelic. My tongue hardened in my mouth and parted through my lips like a heat-seeking missile exiting its silo. I tongued his piss slit. I sucked his head, vacuuming the cheese. He kept his fist wrapped tight below the corona of the head.

"Eat it," he said. "All of it." His passion made him fierce. "Fresse dich!" Not the polite, "Essen sie."

I suctioned his dickhead into my mouth. I beat my own meat, sticking its licentious head out though my own foreskin. Maybe Sebastian had been right about putting down the minister's son. "Probably a neo-Nazi pervert tease." But Dieter definitely wasn't that. He was merely an oversexed village boy with a ten-inch cock and a two-inch foreskin who liked games he could only play with tourists.

"Kneel closer. Open wide." He said it and he smiled. He mounted the parallel bars once more, raising himself effortlessly using only his arms. His strong lean pecs striated. His pink nipples hardened. The light down of golden hair on his body glistened with sweat. As he rose on his magnificent arms, his dick passed my waiting mouth. I almost went for it the way a suckerfish dives for the biggest worm. The kid was tasty, we'd say back in Kansas. He liked to take things slow and easy. He knew the world. He wanted no part of the fast lane, not even on the Bavarian Autobahn. He knew how to savor a moment. We knew we had no more than three times together. My Lufthansa ticket was waiting. We wanted them to count.

Stretched tall above me, held aloft by his arms, he smiled down at me. "I want to kiss you, but from here I can't. Keep your mouth open."

I obeyed.

He worked his rosy cheeks back and forth, his blue eyes shining. He parted his lips and let loose a long strand of gossamer drool start its slow descent from his mouth to mine. No nectar, no champagne, no sacred wine ever tasted better than his spit. I swallowed his juice into me the way I had cleaned the cheese from his foreskin. I know it's become unfashionable and unsafe since, but, back that summer, sex wasn't sex without exchange of bodily fluids. We partied foreskin to butthole.

I hated Sebastian. He was cynical but he was right about vacation romance. Somewhere in the world some radio station was playing Percy Faith's "A Summer

Place" as Dieter began the first of his long slow dips aiming his hard cock deep into my mouth. He was strong as an engine, pistoning his rod deep into my throat.

He made me part of his gymnastics routine.

Rising, pulling his ten-inch cock from my mouth. Lowering, driving his cock deep past my choke point. Starting slowly. Picking up steam. Like a locomotive. Great hard iron wheels slowly moving, driven by the long lateral rods that turn them faster and faster. He picked up the clip of his dips. Sweat poured from his face, his chest, his hairy blond armpits, ran in rivers down to the spout of his cock. Salt-sweat burned my eyes, my throat.

He was what I wanted. He was what I got.

I dived onto his cock, sucked him down tight in my throat, held him captive, pulling on his cock against his strong arms, a tug of war, until he let me win, and dropped to his feet. He took my hair in both his hands and pulled my head back freeing his cock. I gasped for air. His foreskin slipped up tight around his ten-inch cock.

"Now," he said, not letting go of my hair, holding my head in place.

His tight foreskin became the nozzle on a firehose. The long yellow stream blasted my face with all the hyper-force of piss shot through the hose of a boner hardon. His hot wet hardly quenched my fire. He aimed straight for my mouth, and, stilling streaming, rammed his cock down my throat. He was pulsating, near to cuming. My own cock threatened to cum before he did, and, if it shot, I did not know if I could still handle the force of a very young man determined to throat-fuck me silly.

He yanked my hair, pulling my nose deep into his

sweet groin. He was soaked with sweat. I was soaked with piss. He held me in place, and rammed. Rammed. Rammed his cock deep into me. I could feel his foreskin slip and slide over his cock in my mouth. He began groaning. He was close to cuming, and just as I thought he would choke me to death with his huge load of sperm, he pulled out, quickly gripped the tip of his huge foreskin, jerked his cock three times in rapid succession, moaning, grinding his teeth, cuming, not in me, but inside his foreskin. The 'skin ballooned full of his huge dripping load.

"Drink," he said.

I moved in tight next to his foreskin. His fingers released the first sweet taste. I took my cock in my hand.

"Suck my cum from my foreskin," he said.

I put my mouth to the iris eye pinched between his fingers. I put my lips around the cum-balloon of his two-inch 'skin. His fingers were in my mouth. And then they weren't. He released his grip and the whole thick white gelatinous load of his cum, condomed in his foreskin, spilled like burning lava into my mouth. I worked it cheek to cheek, staring up at his great beauty, beating my dick.

"Swallow," he said. "Swallow and cum."

His was an easy order to follow. I swallowed his million clots of seed and shot my own all over his beautifully formed feet, shouting, "Oh, God, Dieter, I'll love you forever! Forever! I will!"

"There you are, you bitch!" The shock was operatic. Abrupt. And very Transylvanian! Sebastian entered the room voice first, fangs second. "*Forever*, for your info, ends with a 9 o'clock flight tonight."

Now I know why hand guns should be outlawed,

ones with silver bullets, to kill the monster bitch Bride of Frankenstein who sits snoring beside me with the remote control tight in his hand.

Nobody crosses the Equator,
on ship or plane,
without initiation by King Neptune.

BILLY BUDD-JONES

When I was 19 in the Merchant Marine, somebody, I don't remember who, one starlit night heading south off the coast of Mexico, told us green young sailors about the Rites of Neptune. He warned us about the initiation of anyone crossing the Equator for the first time. I was laid back in my rack stretching my nice round of bologna, which is what my daddy always called our foreskins—him, me, and my three brothers, all uncut because daddy always said there'd be no circumcision in his family.

Anyway, I was all ears listening to the wise-ass big-talking sailors drooped, half-drunk, around the table under our racks. I didn't much care if they saw me stretching the mouth of my foresnake, or saw me digging my finger deep inside my 3-inch foreskin, my 3-inch cheese-maker, dipping smegma, the way they dipped Copenhagen, tucking it under my lip the same way, because to me nothing tastes better than my mouth tasting like headcheese.

Besides, I have a 7-inch dick flapped with, as I say, a 3-inch flag of ultimate manmeat. Foreskin is a cock's crowning glory. Foreskin is the only thing in the world that makes slick clots of smegma. I never soap the head of my dick inside my foreskin. I always fingerbathe it. When I was a kid and into wrestling and real supple from the sport, I used to be able to bend my back in half like a hairpin and tongue out my foreskin directly. There's no secrets on a merchant vessel. Everybody gets a nickname sooner or later, and mine came real fast. All of them, even the captain, called me "Skin." Every guy in the world has thought about shipping out to see the world and its adventures. All I can say to any man, young or not so, is, I recommend it, but on no less than three ships just to get the real rounded experience.

When we reached the Equator, sure enough, the Rites of Neptune took place as formally as a confirmation or a bar mitzvah. We "Equator Virgins" had no more choice than any Christian or Jewish boys, but the Rites of Neptune were definitely more fun.

The day before we crossed, Neptune's Throne was set up on deck. The Captain grinned down on it all. He was no more than 37 and he had a big enough cock to get behind the festivities. I know. He'd invited me more than once to his cabin. He was Portuguese. An olive-skinned handsome devil with a black moustache, a bristly black crewcut, and like all Portuguese, his bushy black pubic hair nested his fat dick sheathed in an inner-tube of olive foreskin so thick the wrinkles in it shrouded his cockhead so completely the eye of his meat was totally blind. A classic foreskin.

A sailor nick named Queeg won the draw to be King

Neptune. He was a Swede, built like a stone, hung like a drayhorse, and blond as the Viking stock that sired him. When, naked, naked as we all were, he mounted his throne, I saw his big blond cock was leathered with foreskin suitable for a Viking berserker's sword shield. Under the bone-white Equator sun at high noon, Queeg, stamped his staff three times and the games began.

Much of it was foolishness and pot and beer. We were all naked and ordered to grease each other down for a pig wrestle free-for-all. The seasoned sailors stood around the edges of the game. The straight ones tolerated the age-old customs of the sea. The enlightened ones stroked their dicks, sometimes jumping into the pig pile, greasing themselves up. The cook served up a slop special for the occasion and everyone drank from the wooden tubs. The sport wrestling turned to sex wrestling. A bumhole was hardly safe on the greasy deck. Several young sailors were made to sit *en brochette* on the laps of several burly sailors who held them tight, with their cocks up their asses, while their heads were shaved to the skull. In the horseplay, several more sailors were tied down to the deck, playfully but meaningfully, and their chests and crotches shaved. The noon turned into a raucous afternoon, nothing heavy, but plenty of unabashed sex, as if King Neptune and the Equator itself, made permissible and innocent those things sailors most often do at night.

To my surprise, Queeg, who was King Neptune, called out my name. "Skin!" As I approached him across the slippery deck, the Captain, built like a bulldog, joined him at his side. In his hand he held a black leather thong. Queeg stood up. He took my right arm. The Captain my left. They marched me to the center of the deck. The surrounding crowd of sailors cheered. Deftly, Queeg pulled my foreskin forward and the Captain tied it off with the leather thong. My dick hardened immediately. Queeg pulled his own foreskin straightforward and the Captain noosed his cover the same as mine. We were tied together, foreskin to foreskin, and his cock, a good 10 inches, rose to salute mine. Queeg grinned and reached for the Captain's already hard rod and pulled the fat Portuguese foreskin taut. The Captain tied off his own tip. The crowd of sailors cheered. The leather thong triangulated the three of us together. They hardly needed to tell me we were in for a threeway foreskin tug-of-war.

"You've got the Captain," Queeg said.

"You've got King Neptune," the Captain said.

"This is the Equator," I said. "You're no more than two big uncut dicks to me."

They smiled at my smart mouth and I took a step back. Our three foreskins stretched tight. Tough 'skins, all three. We tugged and pulled. Their big bodies outweighed mine, but my 'skin was tougher. The crowd was shouting me the winner; but Queeg and the Captain looked at each other, and, in that peculiar slow-motion of sex remembered, they jumped me, one blond, one dark, and wrestled me to the deck. They knelt over my face and taking their big tied-off cocks in their hands, they stroked their long dongs until first the Captain, and then Queeg, with all his blond muscles ripping, shot their loads into their tied off foreskins that bulged and dripped with cum. To much cheering, first Queeg and then the Captain slowly untied their foreskins and drained them into my open mouth, stretching the eyes of the prepuces, ordering my eager tongue to clean out the three days of cheese they'd each saved for me to eat. The crowd of sailors was chanting, "Smegma! Smegma!"

They would not untie my foreskin, not until late that night it turned out, because, before that, a long line of sailors queued up before me, a select line, only the uncut ones, and it was not just their cum they wanted sucked out. No. Before any of them gave me their cum, I had to dig with my tongue inside the tubes of their foreskins digging cheese from around the sheathed heads of their uncut cocks. Finally, at midnight, my whole body slathered with smegma and my belly full of sailors' cum, the last of them picked me up and carried me to I didn't know where. I was foreskin crazy. I wanted to have wild sex. I wanted to cum. I was 19. I didn't know where I was. Not till I heard them say, "Here's the Foreskin Pig, Captain. He's all yours." And the Captain, taking out his skinning blade, said, "Welcome to the Equator."

Prairie Chicken and
Buckskin Foreskin:
I always been a sucker
for a noble savage.

MY BABY LOVES
THE WESTERN MOVIES!

His buckskin loincloth hung soft an long between his powerful thighs. He was a blond warrior, young, no more n nineteen, with perfect white teeth when he finally smiled. He stood in the prairie clearin sizin up my encampment. His bow an quiver hung from one broad shoulder. He was a good hunter. Two large rabbits, both bucks, hung at his belt. Blood from the kill trickled down through the blond hairs on the inside a his tanned thigh.

He watched me watchin him. I sat stock still on a stump, my legs spread, my own chamois loincloth danglin halfway down to my ankles. His eyes, blue as cornflowers, moved slow up an down my body. I wasn't afraid a him an he wasn't afraid a me or my red beard. We danced a cautious dance. Some tribes the Soldier Blues hadn't made peaceable yet. A man could get killed.

I picked up my knife. His bright blue eyes darted to the sharp blade at his belt, met mine, an relaxed when I no-never-mind started in again whittlin an old stick. Whittlin's good. A man puts a strong chunk a solid wood between his legs an starts workin it an thoughts come into his head something like when he reaches down an takes his own fat cock in his hand, pulls down on the shaft nice an easy an never quite lets his stroke peel his foreskin way back from the head a his cock, until his head pops the 'skin, an blows his white hot flume. Thinkin those thoughts raised my lodge pole, tentin out my loincloth.

His keen eyes measured my barely covered hardon. Slowly, he moved his hand over the soft buckskin a his own loincloth. He wanted what I wanted. I surveyed him once more from his roughout moccasin boots, laced up tight around his hard calves, to his washboard belly an hard chest. His smooth blond skin was tanner n berry juice. A thin leather lace banded his head a flowin blond hair. His cock hung big an bent, tryin to jut up an out through the buckskin that pouched his nakedness in the front an gathered into the crack running up his rear. I figured he had been stole as a blond child an raised by Indians, a not uncommon adventure, an he was just old enough a brave to be wonderin what white men was all about.

I hoped his real pa had the sense not to let his ma cut him, an ruin him, takin his foreskin from him. Folks like that go and call Indians heathens. Ain't nothin like a good foreskin, redskin or whiteskin, blackskin or brownskin, when the right brave is brave enough an good-lookin enough to tickle my fancy which is located for ticklin at the back a my throat. I always been a sucker for a noble savage.

What I had standin before me was a genuine wild-child, blond-child, man-child whose strong hand touched first one dark nipple an then stroked over the bear-claw necklace, hanging across his pectorals, an then down his belly, jumpin the waistband a his breechclout, until his sinewy hand rested cupped aroun what looked to me to be a goodsize piece a uncut blond prairie chicken.

He was uncut. I knew for certain. My dick always hardens near hidden uncut meat the way a dowsin rod twitches over water runnin under a parched prairie.

Ogallala Sioux, I figured, had raised him. So I suspected he spoke some trader English, even if he didn't much remember how he talked before he was carried off, but I wasn't interested in palaver. I was interested in siphonin out his foreskin with my tongue to get some prairie cheese to eat with my prairie meat.

Folks call me a trapper for less n they know what I really trap. They buy skins from me, but they ain't no cash money in the territory can buy the kind a manskins I hunt down an trap. I'm a buckskinner chasin foreskin.

Sometimes a man hunts best just sittin on a stump in the middle a his own camp, stripped down to breechclout an boots, a jug a strong apple jack at his side, rollin his own smoke, carvin pieces a wood into what some call "Widow's Comforters," an what I call woodcocks, carved in medicine shapes, with uncut heads, an smooth enough for a man to slide up inside hisself when the plains night is clear an starry bright an lonelier than the frozen face a the moon.

The blond brave was bold.

Before I could motion him into camp, he came stridin toward me, his heels kickin up little clouds of dust. He was a handsome warrior brave. He could be dangerous, but so could I. We both were chancin it. I been a trader for twelve years, since I was almost sixteen. I seen men at their best an at their worst an generally like em somewhere in between, which is where we were when he came an stood four foot in front a me, dropped his rabbits, like he was tradin with me, an lifted the flap on his breechclout, tuckin it up in his belt, exposing the warm chamois skin pouched around his big balls an uncut horsecock.

The skin a his breech was worn so smooth over his goods, my own cockhead slid like a one-eyed snake through my own foreskin. I could see the outline a his uncut horse 'skin shieldin his cock. I humored my fancy that his Indian name was "Horse Skin." I reckoned he hadn't come to powwow. He had one thing on his mind. No big blond boy, raised so bold an wild, was gonna walk right up an stand almost between my legs so we could flap our jaws, when we could jaw our 'flaps. Sure as shootin he weren't no Indian. He looked like he might a been outa some a that strong blond German stock that settled a long way's hard ride north an east, farther even than the Dakotas.

He snorted air from his nostrils. Like a horse.

I reached out an touched the big pouch a his breechclout. He took a step closer. He put his hand on my naked shoulder. I looked up at him an he squinted his skyblue eyes, then he smiled, but his lips never parted. He put his hand on the back a my head, a gesture that in these parts can give a white man with a full scalp a red hair somethin've a palpitation. Kinda nervous, I sniffed through his buckskin the rich smell a unwashed cock, that pure, wild scent a unwashed cock that's so healthy a man like me remembers why he left civilization in the first place.

I turned my face an rubbed my red beard on the back a his hand. He touched my cheek with his palm. I figgered he was curious about how he might grow up, like a white man, different from the Indians. For a young blond, he was yet as smooth and hairless as the Indians who adopted him. But I could tell on his cheeks, under his armpits, an especially by the light line a hair arrowing down from his chest to his navel, that he was gonna be furred heavy when he grew up. Probably never leave his wild Indian ways behind. Never be civilized either. Be halfway round-eye an halfway Indian. An neither a both. The best kind. Most likely grow up to be one a them lone-wanderin moutainmen, like I become, trappin 'skins.

The way he looked at me made me feel my mouth was the answer to a question his dick was askin.

I reached for the cinch on the belt a his breechclout. I hesitated. I looked up at him an my mouth musta fell open starin up at the kid. He smiled, curlin his lip, with just that edge a meanness I find excitin when it ain't no real cowtown brawl. Then he let drip with the longest, whitest, sweetest tastin, droolin spit I coulda ever asked for. He moved in over my open mouth an I swear the spit a his honey was no thicker than those white webs that float through the air in Indian summer. The long flow from his mouth to mine juiced my skinner's cock up harder. I sucked his spit into my mouth an we both smiled cuz, without so much as a word, we figgered out who was gonna play chief.

He raised his lean muscled arms in the air holdin his bow in one hand, his medicine pouch in the other. He raised his face to the sky. His long blond hair hung down his back. Sweat from his pits ran down his dusty tanned body. He sang out three times the name a the Great Spirit. I pulled the cinch at his tight waist, an his breechclout floated away down his powerful runner's legs.

He was buck naked, starin at the blue sky hummin over the bone-white plains. Rabbit blood ran red down his inner thigh, pinkin with his sweat, evaporatin in the heat. I licked it away with my tongue.

His young horse cock hung between my eyes. His meat was half hard, but the shaft a it, untouched by him or me, was arollin, side to side, growin, stretchin down the long corridor a the biggest flag a foreskin I ever did see a man run up his pole.

I touched its iris eye with my fingers. It was softer n doeskin. Liftin him up by his 'skin, I raised his thickenin dick toward my nose, breathin in the wild smell a his young cock. I pulled the big nipple a 'skin through my moustache. His body arched back like a bow. I kissed his foreskin. I sniffed it, tongued it, nipped it, sucked it. His risin cock aimed straight arrow up his belly. Indians maybe raised him, but in the big bow a his crotch, his meat was fat, big, blond German sausage. His balls climbed over each other beggin to blow like a horse soldiers' ammo dump stashed too near a redhot cannon.

He sucked in a deep breath. His body was a natural wonder. I've heard a Indian rock climbers who coulda scaled his torso pullin themselves up with nothin but their fingertips clawin up in the tight crevasses a his chiseled belly.

He put his arms behind his head an untied the thin leather thong a his headband. He craned his head forward, an looked about to dive mouth-first down on his own hard cock pointin straight up his belly. My hand cupped his balls at the base a his cock. He reached down an braided his fingers into mine, workin me an his tips together in a slow tease up his shaft. Our twenty fingers met at the tip a his foreskin. His growin cock was still hardenin. He guided my fingers, both thumbs and both forefingers, to grip the top a his foreskin the way a man grips a boot before shovin his foot into it. He wanted me to stare down into the openin iris a meaty darkness. He had everythin.

Horse balls.

Horse cock.

Horse 'skin.

I held his big flap a palomino foreskin tight in my fingers, stretchin his cock out real easy from his groin, while he wrapped the brown thong a his headband tight as a wampum pouch between the tip a his foreskin an the head a his cock. Expert, he tied off the eye to his foreskin with a perfect slip knot. All the time his cock was advancin up from its roots, slidin up the inside tube a his tied-off 'skin like a stiff lodgepole workin up inside a buckskin teepee. He held the long laces a his knotted headband in his hands like they was reins to the wild horsecock he moved left an right, guidin his tied rawhide raw hide toward my mouth.

Nothin slides down a grown man's throat like uncut dick.

He rode my face, guidin his huge cock down my throat, chokin me with the flapped tip a foreskin. He tasted young an wild churnin into my face lettin me go loco wolfin on the saltlick taste a his sweaty blond meat.

The rawhide rasped my throat, cut the corners a my mouth, an kept his dick hooded.

He worked me hard. The sun beat down on us. I fell back on my elbows an he followed me down. I ripped my own uncut cock free a my breech. With one hand I stripped my tight foreskin back farther exposin my cockhead to the hot sun. I rubbed my hands over the smooth hard haunches a his oily blond butt, wettin my fingers, an slicked my palm down my shaft. He reached back an ran his finger smooth around the inside a my foreskin. His finger pulled up clotted with my fresh churnin cheese. He studied the white clots with his blue eyes, posed almost for a tintype, then shoved his finger in his mouth an sucked it clean.

Always trust a blond Indian.

He slowly withdrew his dick from my mouth. He leaned over me, an smilin, drooled down the long web mixed outa my 'skin cheese an his spit. I squished the nectar through my teeth. I stored it in my cheeks. He knelt up over me, lean an wild against the noon sky, knees straddlin my chest, big cock, still tied off blind, risin hardon. No stoppin us. Whoever he was, he was "Horse Skin" to me now. Takin the reins a his headband, he aimed his cock past my lips, across my teeth, an rode on in. We was different nations but we had the same notions. Whatever Sun Dance foreskin-ritual this young man called Horse Skin had endured as a boy called Pony Skin, he had emerged a warrior, an his sturdy cock was his lance.

He was hung so big my back-door wanted him to slam me a good poke, but he had other ideas. He rode me, his knees astraddle my chest, gaggin me with his dick, gettin a might forceful, jammin the thick nipple a his foreskin deep down my throat. My eyes watered. Without missin a slam he looked down at me, bared his teeth, smilin, an grunted.

He had me where he wanted me: on my back between his legs with his dick sheathed in his tied-off foreskin slidin in, an pullin outa, my throat, but we were equal cuz I had him where I wanted him too.

He gritted his teeth. He was drillin for the kill. He looked down at me through the long blond hair fallin straight down aroun his chiseled face. Deep in his blue eyes I saw the ancient sacred bows cock, each armed with the fierce arrows a bloodlust. His eyes aimed straight into mine. He drove his savage cock, its blind eye tied shut, hard into me. The blond German boy had disappeared. The warrior Horse Skin had taken his place.

I raised my hands to touch his face, to call him back to civilization. His hands, savage, grasped my wrists to stop me. He bucked up, his dick keepin me, impaled, on my back. He dived forward over my face, still holding my hands, stretchin them out spreadeagle in the hot dust. He was strong with the strength a hard cock. He was strong with the strength a combat born a endless naked wrestlin matches with the young bucks a his tribe. He was unstoppable, but I made a show a strugglin against him, to show him I was no squawman, to show him I knew how to wrestle a strong brave in the games a love. My resistance excited him. He drove deeper, harder. I opened wider, breathin gasps, suckin in his drivin cock, his hard belly slammin down into my face, sweat from his crotch drippin down into my eyes an beard, his balls bangin against the outside a my throat filled on the inside with his cock.

My head lay back in the dirt. My eyes were runnin tears from the burnin a his sweatin drippin on me, an from my chokin. I couldn't even touch my own dick afraid I'd shoot before him an then what would I do, so I opened my throat futher an I received his big horse 'skinned dick, acceptin him inside my insides, where I wanted him an his wild seed. I fell back under his weight, knowin a Kiowa medicine man told me once I had powerful medicine if I only knew how to find it. I remembered the Kiowa taught me my inner Eye, so I took my Eye inside my throat, watchin his big, long, thick-veined cock slidin hard down the sleeve a my throat, back past my choke-flap, back past my breathin, back where his horse cock could bury his foreskin head deep inside my body.

Sand stuck in my hair an to my back an butt. Horse Skin, stud-fuckin me, glowed. His sweat caught the comin noon light a the prairie like a crest. His hair, yellow as the sun, an his body, blond-brown, rose weightless over me. This was good medicine. This is what the Kiowa holy man had meant.

Horse Skin lunged his cock down deep inside my face. I felt its hard head, wrapped in tied 'skin, burrow past the cave a my mouth down the long tunnel a my throat. I was the earth an he was the sky. My dark recesses opened to his penetratin blond light. He coulda killed me. I coulda died a happy man. But he was no renegade, an I knew I was gonna live happy on the memory a this all my days forever.

I opened wider. He drove deeper. He made small gruntin sounds, then blew faster puffs a air, fuckin faster. I felt his 'skin-covered cockhead grow bigger inside his tied-off foreskin like some huge medicine-gourd ram. My

own cock at hard attention bobbed an weaved, an a run
a clear gleat ran from the teardrop eyehole a my own foreskin down my cock. I ached to touch it, but his strong
hands still pinioned me under all the weight a his buck-
in body. His grunts grew louder, risin over the quiet early noon a the hummin prairie, until he was whoopin,
strainin, yawpin, an cumin inside the tied sheath a his
'skin, inside my throat. I felt his sweet juice balloon up
behind the knot tyin off his 'skin. I wanted the explosion
a his manseed chokin my throat, floodin my mouth, me
gulpin an burblin an suckin the white clots across my
tongue an teeth, tastin him the way a wine merchant nips
his lips over his wares, but instead his knotted foreskin
stayed thick as buckskin between me an his seed. All I
tasted was a trickle a blood from my nose he didn't mean
to bump so hard, he was so young, slammin into the dirt
my head impaled on his cock.

Still quiverin, Horse Skin knelt upright over me on
his knees straddlin my chest, with his cock drippin spit
all over my face. His long shaft, topped off with his foreskin balloonin out with cream, hung over me like a club.
He looked down at me, both a us pantin, my hands tryin
to find my cock around his sinewy legs, an suddenly with
both hands, he grabbed the rawhide reins a his headband
wrapped aroun the very tip a his foreskin, an gave em a
yank that slipped the knot to a spill.

The fast splat a his cum splurted through the hot
air, splungin, burnin across my face, fillin my eyes an
nose an gaspin mouth, my tongue wagglin up into the
tasty rain drenchin me in hot fire. I gurgled an tasted,
not just cum from his horse cock, but cum fucked up an
stored in his horse 'skin. He leaned forward, put his

hands aroun my throat, an stared down into my eyes, wantin me to swallow, with his hands on the outside squeezin closed the throat he had so carefully fucked open.

His was the noblesse oblige a foreskin.

I swallowed down my throat with his hands ringin, but not quite wringin, my neck. He was terrible excitin. His thighs kept my hands from my cock the way his hands had held my arms pinioned.

He wanted me to cum. I wanted to cum. He dribbled fresh spit from his sweet mouth. He turned to sunlight as noon rose true above us. His hands left my throat an his blond silhouette rose lean an erect between me an the sun. In his shadow, I watched the head a his cock retreat inside his big foreskin the way the moon eclipses the sun. He lowered the three-inch tip a his 'skin at the end a his long cock to my lips an I suckled him the way a man suckles another man, tonguin out his cum juices, drinkin his sweat, swallowin the deep rivers flowin beneath the parched prairie.

I knew how things was supposed to be, an my dick, untouched, shot, shootin up. Light white arrows arched into the blue air from my throbbin cock.

We smoked his pipe an lay naked next to one another on a blanket in the shade a my tent, me holdin his big blond foreskin in my hand, not wantin him to go, when, come dusk, with bow over his shoulder, an one rabbit on his belt, he strode off, blond as all getout, into the prairie darkness, giftin me with one buck rabbit for my supper.

Historical Note

Mountain men were different critters. This country had never seen their likes before. Distinguished by their buckskin clothing, Indian beads, long hair often plaited with feathers, the mountain men, like James Fenimore Cooper's Leatherstocking and Robert Redford's *Jeremiah Johnson*, lived out their wild lifestyle on the great plains and high in the Rockies. These men were hearty souls keeping one jump ahead of the tame civilization that followed them. They left society and females behind in their pursuit of the rugged romance of a male life dedicated to partnering with another man in a bond that could only be cut by whiskey or greed or lust or death.

President Jefferson's Louisiana Purchase of 1804, and the subsequent expedition by Lewis and Clark, are what actually started the movement to the West. By 1806, the tales brought back by Lewis and Clark of a magnificent, rich land sparked erotic imaginations everywhere. Adventurers who answered this call to primitive excitement were to become what are now called mountain men.

Their rugged buckskin breed is not dead and gone. At the millennium, mountain men still very much live among us, a couple thousand or so full-time, a couple hundred thousand who live the buckskin life on weekend encampments all over the west and northwest, keeping the mountain man tradition of tipis, smoky fires, leather, beards, and black powder rifles alive much the same as other groups of hearty American men gather together in their uniforms to re-enact our Revolutionary and Civil wars.

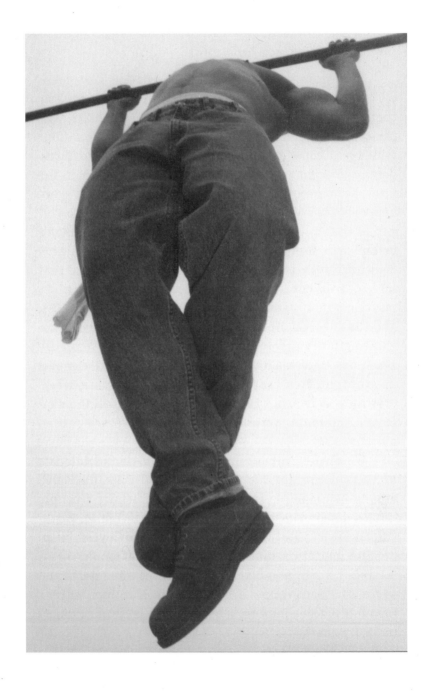

Cinema Blues:
He was one of those people
who belong inside a movie theater.

THE UNSEEN HAND
IN THE LAVENDER LIGHT

REEL ONE
His life was a silent movie.

His mind craved flickers the way his mouth watered over salt-grit popcorn. In the early Forties, while the World War raged from Europe to the Pacific, the doll-faced waitress who was his mother snapped her gum in downtown Peoria's famous Bee Hive Cafe while she fielded her counter tips into an issue-by-issue collection of *Photoplay* magazine which he read between the daily double features.

Each afternoon she paid his nine-cent admission to the Apollo Theater. Each dinner time, after the matinee double bill, he left the balcony to eat supper on the last counter stool at the Bee Hive, and thought it not at all odd that his mother's regulars called her "Countess Betty" because she never waited tables, always working the faster turnover of the counter.

She flirted with the men from the County Court House across Main Street, and the factory workers from Caterpillar. She turned nickel tips into quarters. The War Department had retooled Caterpillar Tractor Company into a defense plant. Peoria, in the middle of nowhere, became strategic. Landing Ship Tank Boats, built up the Illinois River, cruised downstream past Peoria, with soldiers waving, sometimes coming ashore, headed for the war. The nightly blackouts and air-raid drills made everyone feel important. The Caterpillar men, exempt from the draft, built Army trucks and heavy equipment. He liked them—more than he could say—calling his mother "Betty Grable." She was their very own Countess of the Counter Stools.

She was the star of the Bee Hive Cafe. No one even knew her real name was Helen which was the only name she let him call her, and only in private in their rented room above the Pour House Tavern where, tired from gabbing all day long under a war poster warning "Loose Lips Sink Ships," she wanted no talking at all, taking off her shoes and her makeup, and watching out the window the soldiers and sailors leaning in the lamplight and whistling at the girls going in and out of the Pour House.

His mother, a take-charge arranger nobody dared cross, saw to his free meals the way she arranged his evening admission to the Apollo with the manager, a young man come downstate from Chicago to learn the ropes of the movie theater business. His weak eyesight kept him from the draft and kept the movies on screen out of focus. One way or another, his mother was sure, even with a "Four-Eyes" 4-F man, a living was to be had in the movies, if not on the screen, then behind it.

Beggars, she shouted over her busy shoulder to her customers, and she meant herself, can't be choosers. Some people, he had heard her say to new waitresses, are born to be actors and some are just plain born to be the audience.

She never spoke directly to him.

Anything she had to say to him he overheard her telling someone else.

He got the point. He looked like his father.

She knew their place in life, his and hers, and she vaguely shamed him, too old for baby-sitters and too young for the draft, fending for him until he could fend for himself. He knew she wanted to divorce his father who was somewhere off in the war, but she was too patriotic to write him a "Dear John." So she acted, vague, like she was no longer married, and ambiguous, like her husband was dead, which was a convenience of war and the real hope behind her pretty doll's face.

No matter. He got the point his father had probably always missed. His mother, only fifteen years older than him, was a star, but despite her Hollywood longings during the endless war in Europe and the Pacific, none of the slick succession of young managers ever took her away or even convinced the home office in Chicago to install sound in the silent grind-house of the Apollo.

He longed to walk around the corner of Main and Jefferson to the brightly lit jewel of the Rialto Theater where big Hollywood pictures blazed across the silver screen in Technicolor and thundering sound. But his mother could not arrange things at the Rialto.

So he had sat, stuck in the Apollo, staring at the mute screen, out-of-fashion, out-of-sync, under the clack of the silent projectors. Even before he could read the dialog on screen, he had learned, without even trying, to read lips. He found no contradiction that the written dialog often said one thing while the actors said something else. He began pretending he heard words coming from their moving mouths, not knowing his mother was making arrangements and cooing sounds, with whoever was manager that month, behind the tatty screen where pigeons perched on the high dusty beams of the tired old Apollo.

Then quite suddenly, because of the war shortages, everyone said, the Apollo went dark. He was the last one left standing in the empty lobby. At the Bee Hive, his mother sighed something almost grateful about the end of that flea pit that should be sold for scrap, but within a month the Chicago owners had sent in what his mother, leaning close into her mirror to tweeze her arched eyebrows, called, with a sneer, a Rosie-the-Riveter team of women painters and carpenters who remodeled the old girl, because movies, with the war and all, were bigger box office than ever.

Sitting alone in the balcony of the new Apollo the night of its grand reopening, he thought he had died and gone to an Arabian palace in heaven. The handsome new manager, another 4-F flat-footed floogie with a floy-floy, so his mother, always scoring laughs at the Bee Hive, reported, turned on the new projectors, and with the blaring sound track came the 1944 *Pathé News of the World*: a blitzkrieg montage of world leaders, beauty pageants, faceless troops, crazy inventions, atrocities, circus acts, advice on spotting saboteurs and spies, and fashion-ration tips, narrated by a man's enthusiastic voice, showing pretty young women drawing a line with an eyebrow pencil straight up the middle of the back of their long bare legs to create the illusion of a hosiery seam in a world that had run out of nylons.

Everyone was war-crazy.

He was too young to be of any more use than collecting tin cans and lard from patriotic housewives even in the last desperate year of rationed gas and food shortages. He lived out the world-nightmare in the balcony of the Apollo, the hundred lights of its marquee strategically blacked out. He liked the friendly way the newsreel soldiers, who danced wild athletic jitter-bug contests, hugged each other. But the violent exploding newsreel battles scared him. The bombed rubble of destroyed cities frightened him. The long lines of refugees in rags, trudging icy roads past burning tanks, shocked him because they looked like him. The tortured children hung up by their thumbs terrified him. The shot, grotesque, frozen dead bodies petrified him. Each week the newsreels grew more bloodcurdling.

The audience around him was weeping.

The Apollo was sobbing.

Women and men.

And him. Alone in his seat. Crying in the balcony.

He felt there was only one finale to these real news movies between the feature movies. In the mad world of war, both sides were going to kill each other until no one was left. He was so scared the exploding World War, no one could end, was about to spin out of control, about to leap off the screen, leap out of Europe, leap out of the Pacific, that night after night he woke wet with dreams of breathless gagging sickening panic.

The news from the front was so bad, the patrons of the Bee Hive grew strangely quiet. Behind the counter, even his mother shut up. Then, as if by force of collective will, the terror ended.

Suddenly, in the next wet April spring, the war in Europe was over. Even more suddenly, the following muggy August, the war in the Pacific ended with a surprising blast of radiant energy that made grown-ups cry with gratitude. People, screaming, laughing, joyous, crying, dancing, drinking, celebrating, filled the streets of Peoria, crowded shoulder to shoulder, traffic stopped, toilet paper unrolling out of office windows, horns blaring, singing, hugging, kissing, walking across cars stalled in the human surge of happiness into the streets, delirious, unlike anything he had seen, so happy, they were, he was, the fear gone, sitting by himself on top of a car under the marquee of the Apollo Theater whose lights in broad afternoon blazed away in rolling electric waves of American glory and joy and freedom with one word the Apollo manager himself had hung in huge letters: PEACE!

Then one suppertime, later that hot August after VE Day and VJ Day, he sat eating alone at the Bee Hive. It surprised him not at all that the waitress who was his mother just upped and casually vanished.

The last he saw of her she was carting a tray of four lip-sticked soda glasses through the double-doors of the sweltering kitchen.

She disappeared deeper into the cooking steam each time the doors, one fanning in as the other fanned out, clipped each other to shorter and shorter arcs.

Finally, the energy of her push evaporated and the doors seamed to a halt.

It made equal sense later that evening to find a new manager at the Apollo, a stern-faced woman whose steely-clipped hair told him without being asked that she had never heard about arranging his admission. He stood back from her and considered that since he at fifteen knew nothing of life, he must watch the movie-shows to find how people lived. The waitress who was his mother had never talked to him and all that was left of the man she named as his father was an eight-inch red vinyl record with sounds of someone laughing and whistling and trying to sing "Amapola" like he was dying drunk at long distance in a far-off phone booth.

Through the box-office glass he saw the stern-jawed woman point to him under the marquee, as if he were skulking, which he wasn't, not till she pointed at him, and then he could not help starting to skulk he was so embarrassed, because no one had ever pointed at him before, not even his teachers.

No one had ever noticed him.

The woman, who looked like the woman who had been foreman of the Rosie Riveters, said something he could not hear to the ticket girl who squinted her eyes to look at him. She said something back to the woman who pursed her lips, raised her chin, and humphed approval that someone at least knew his face.

He wasn't nobody. He was the audience.

She smiled at him.

Embarrassed, he shoved his hands into his corduroys, but he could not turn his back on the celestial bright of the marquee. He was one of those people who belong inside a movie theater.

In that moment's pause he decided he must arrange

things for himself. The woman smiled again and he walked toward her the way a camera approaches a movie actor. The patrons in line, had they watched, could have seen them talking behind the heavy glass doors of the lobby. The woman led him across the new red movie carpet into her office. Ten minutes later he emerged in black slacks striped down the side with satin. He wore a maroon jacket which was a size too large and he carried a flashlight. The woman touched her hands to her hair and pointed him toward the balcony. A living, the waitress who was his mother had said, was to be made in the movies.

REEL TWO
Transformations.

He was a bumper, a toucher, one of those kids who can't make it through a store without fingering every pencil and pen and magazine within reach. He grew to expect the clerks to follow him. He wanted one of them, particularly the one whose badge read "Mr. Coates," to collar him and take him to the security room of Clark's Department Store, second-best to Block and Kuhl's Department Store. He wanted desperately for Mr. Coates to accuse him of shoplifting. He wanted the police to be called and he wanted to be stripped down to his fifteen-year-oldness and searched and proven innocent. He wanted people to look at him and see he had never taken anything that was not his, or even laid claim to anything that was. But as it was, no one thought he had anything that was stolen, or even somehow remarkably different, and the very distinguished Mr. Coates never said a word. He simply shot his cuffs efficiently down over the black hair on his thick wrists and ignored the boy he knew as the usher from the aisles of the Apollo Theatre.

He spoke to no one except the moviegoers who asked for the time of the next feature or the direction to the loge or the lounge. Every night of his life with the waitress he had spent at the movies, so it had never occurred to him to ask for a night out when the manager herself made the suggestion. He did not argue. He pulled off his maroon jacket and hung his flashlight in the cabinet inside her office door. She smiled at him and handed him two passes.

"Perhaps," she said, "there is a pretty little someone you can take to the show."

He shook his head. She was deliberately confusing him. He knew she was right, suggesting that he ought to do what other people do. He had watched a million movie dates and it ought to have helped him. But somehow he hadn't the click for it.

He was no dummy.

He had ushered the balcony long enough to watch the back rows while on screen two lovers kissed in the evening mist and the world stood still except for trains rushing into tunnels and trees bending in the wind and waves crashing on shore. Enough glow spilled from the triangle of light shooting from the small window of the projection booth down to the screen. He had orders to stop anyone from getting fresh in the balcony, but he could never bring himself to flash his light into the snuggles of couples who learned fast enough that when he was the usher no one would bother them. From his station at the top of the balcony aisle, he watched over the audience and stared down at the screen.

During the rolling credits at the end of each feature, he opened the doors. Slightly disheveled couples pulled themselves together, whisking powder off suit-jacket lapels and patting hair into place. They filed out through a long gauntlet of new couples held back by his red velvet chain. Some customers entered the balcony alone. One, a woman who reminded him of his waitress, regularly tipped him ten cents for showing her to the seat he saved for her each Tuesday for the last double feature.

An evening to himself threw him for a loss.

He lingered longer than usual at the Bee Hive, where the owner, sorry for him that the waitress who was his mother had disappeared into the steam of the kitchen, had allowed him to arrange his own discount meal ticket.

He pinched three paper straws from bottom to top. He alternated the pinches at right angles one above the other. He said she-loves-me and she-loves-me-not and never once wondered who the she was as long as she did more than she didn't. He reached for a fourth straw, but the waitress, who was not at all like his mother, playfully slapped his hand.

"Those cost money," she said. She pulled his empty plate away. Her name was Crystal. "More java?" she asked.

He looked at her and felt the two passes in his pocket. He smiled and she poured the strong boiled coffee up to the green ring around the outside lip of his heavy china cup.

She looked possible.

A wisp of blonde hair escaped from her black snood. Her lips were red as Technicolor. She looked like she could use a movie.

He smiled again.

"Want some pie?" she asked, knowing he missed her teasing double meaning.

He decided to ask her. He could take her past the box office, through the lobby, and up the stairs to the balcony. Unless maybe she wouldn't go to the balcony. Unless, maybe, this first time, they ought to sit in the loge.

"Well, do you, or don't you?" she said. Her hand made a petulant little fist on her aproned hip.

He smiled and held up his passes.

She stepped toward him. "Gee," she said, bussing up his glass of bent straws.

He handed them closer to her.

She was definitely balcony.

"You work there, don'tcha."

He tried staring directly into her eyes, but she looked straight at the passes. Like a hypnotist, he waved them back and forth and closer to her face.

She blinked, took the passes from his hand, and kissed them a light hello as she breezed them into her pocket full of tips. "Thanks," she said. "Here I always thought you were a pretty odd guy, always standing in the back of the balcony, watching everything that goes on up there. Shows how wrong a girl can be."

He felt the blood rush to his face. He wanted to say that was not what he had meant at all. The passes were not her tip. His breath seemed gone and the walls of the Bee Hive seemed to split at the seams and fall back and she kept wiping the counter around his coffee cup as if he were her best customer ever.

"I spent my last dollar on this really cute gold ankle

bracelet at the dimestore," she said. "It was a dollar-nineteen, but I split everything with my best girlfriend Angela."

He reached for his coffee to hide his face and make it small behind the cup as he tilted it to his mouth.

"I'll get to wear it tonight since I got these two tickets to the show."

He set his cup down in the saucer and wished for a director who would yell "Cut!"

"Here's a piece of pie," she whispered, sliding a fork into his fingers. "I'll forget it on your check."

He slid backwards off the counter stool.

"You don't want the pie?"

He pulled the correct change from his black usher's slacks and laid it on the counter. He slipped from the Bee Hive into the street.

"Brother, what a jerk!" she said, just loud enough for him to doubt he heard it.

Down the block, under the Apollo marquee, the crowd from the early show eddied out to the sidewalk on Main Street. Men with girls on their arms paused in mid-stride to light up. Couples swirled out the doors around the obedient row of patrons waiting entry to the next double feature. Clusters of moviegoers slowed him. He pushed his way through. He saw a man in a gold gabardine sport shirt. He accidentally on purpose bumped into him. The man said, "Watch it, kid!" Overhead two bulbs had burnt out in the marquee. They broke the illusion of the long running line of light.

No one ever noticed that he walked into people he needed to touch. Bumping was his only intimacy. Since his mother had disappeared into the kitchen of the Bee

Hive, no one had come up the stairs above the Pour House to their small room with the single sink, the In-a-Door bed, and the old horsehair sofa where he had slept before she had vanished. No one touched him but the barber at the Barber College where he sat high in a chair every Saturday, between mirrors curving off to infinity, watching his hair clippings fall onto the sheet pinned tight around his neck and draped over his shoulders and arms and knees like a tent hiding his hands in his lap. So he had settled for bumps, as if could nudge off anonymous elbows and backs atoms and energy, as if he could learn through a bump, which strangers thought the accident of a clumsy boy, how it felt with someone else. His eye was a camera snapping fantasy people for footage he projected in his head late at night, laid flat out and alone between the sheets of the Murphy bed, listening to the shouts and singing downstairs in the Pour House, holding his private self hard in hand.

But this night he purposely touched no one. He darted through the doors of the Apollo, waved to the doorman, and headed straight up the stairs to the balcony. He folded himself into the last row of seats. He slouched down on the middle of his back and hooked the indentation in each kneecap onto the curved back rim of the seat in front of him. The empty screen reflected the soft glow of the intermission houselights. Every ten feet down both side walls hung amber globes, each with a hand-painted lady, bathing identically, her towel draped like bunting across her torso.

He had never seen the balcony so empty. A good double bill kept the few Monday night moviegoers on the main floor. He heard them settling into their seats. The murmur of their conversation climbed up the moorish lattice stenciled on the walls. Their voices gathered to a vast hum under the domed ceiling where violet light hidden indirectly behind the lip of the lower circumference of the dome mixed their human voices into an indistinguishable hum. He fixed his eyes on the hypnotic purple light that grew iridescent as the other house lights dimmed. The sharp light from the projection booth cut over his head, but the movie that night held no interest. He did not even take his eyes off the violet dome to look down at the screen as the violet and purple dome melted to lavender.

Some sense in his body told him he was about to defy gravity.

Only the crick in his neck and the pressure from the inner-spring cushion under his back seemed to hold him in his seat.

He wrapped his arms through the arms of the seat.

Staring up at the soft lavender light, he lost time and direction.

A moment of panic swept through him followed by ineffable pleasure.

He imagined himself falling up, up, up into the pool of violet light, floating unnoticed above the moviegoers, lazy and dreamy, until the intimate unseen hand, inflating and then letting go the neck of a balloon, reddened the violet, shocking the audience who craned their necks and pointed to see him ricocheting insanely off the ceiling and walls, growing smaller and smaller until he disappeared.

He had never been chloroformed but he felt it was much like this.

The unseen hand lifted, and a dark mass next to him, almost invisible to his eyes blinded with the dome's lavender brightness, rose softly and moved, he could not be bothered in his swoon to remember, either up or down the aisle. He woke from what he had recognized as not sleep. Like a man who starts suddenly during a sermon, he looked left and right to see if anyone had noticed.

He did not know how much time had passed or even the difference between what might have happened and what he might have imagined. The balcony was still nearly empty. He untangled his arms and sat up straight in his seat. The second feature had begun, and he felt with little curiosity that the sticky wet on his undershorts was growing chill near the open zipper that he had not opened. Ten rows ahead of him sat the nearest patron. It was the lady who usually tipped him the ten cents. Five seats from her he spied Crystal and, he guessed, her friend Angela. In the first row, his feet propped up on the balcony railing, he was sure he saw Mr. Coates sitting in a blue halo of cigarette smoke. When had these people arrived? Then he remembered the door at the top of the aisle opening and closing during his doze, and he thought no more about it, because he was used to the way people appeared and disappeared.

REEL THREE
Some nights you wake up screaming.

After he graduated from school and his job at the Apollo, he found other theaters, other cities. He moved upstate

to Chicago. The movies widened from 35mm to 70mm
Cinemascope. They left him breathless. He panicked the
first time he noticed it. He panicked and gulped in a quart
of air. He had sat through a feature and a half before he
realized that he was forgetting to breathe. He had
thought everyone breathed automatically, but somehow
he was forgetting and he panicked. He stood up in his
balcony seat and walked up the steps of the long carpet-
ed aisle. He felt he would never make it. He vowed he
must stop going up to the balconies. He pushed open the
doors to the lobby with a great effort and brushed the arm
of a blonde woman carrying a medium popcorn and a
large Coke. His gasping lungs filled with her raggy scent.
He felt sick. How could he forget to breathe? He had
sloshed her Coke. He left her damning him in his wake.
Outside, down the street from the running lights of the
marquee, he leaned against a mailbox and looked up at
the cold moon rising over Lake Michigan. He wanted ten
deep breaths, but he counted only six before the freezing night air hurt his throat. An elevated train rattled
past overhead. He shivered and turned from the moon
to the marquee.

An usher had climbed up a tall wooden ladder with
a box full of large plastic letters. One week's bill gave way
to another as the usher slid the letters around on their
wire tracks. While the usher struggled with the film titles, gibberish hung on the Bryn Mawr Theater's glow-
ing marquee. He remembered that a couple years before
it had been himself up on such a ladder, spelling and
spacing words for everyone to read. The flush of altitude
sickness from the balcony burned in his gut and he
turned, on that barricaded edge of not-knowing that is

the edge of self-revelation, and walked away.

"Moonlight," he wrote on a scrap of paper in his pocket, "has the same believability as black-and-white film. The moon washes the color from everything. Landscapes and faces lose their tint. Everything becomes believable within the range of gray."

Even one's self.

As a part-time projectionist, living on popcorn, he had worked his way through college and into graduate school and had taken to writing while he walked, insomniac through lonely nights, hanging out in tiled coffee shops with fluorescent waitresses. Sometimes when there was snow blanketing and silencing the Near North Side of Chicago, the night waitresses would have mercy on him and for his dime pour him bottomless cups of coffee and call him Shakespeare because of his books and his glasses, but he would not really think of them as real until later when he thanked them ever-so because the air was cold on his shivering hand as he emptied his bladder under the El, signing his melting yellow autograph into banks of pure white snow. What he wrote on paper was secret and wonderful. He kept it, at the coffee-shop counters, covered with one hand and only read it himself when back in his rented room that was not unlike the room that his mother the waitress had so long before abandoned.

He could no longer remember her face and it disturbed him slightly, because the face of anyone named Helen should have launched a thousand ships. He could identify the profile of a long-since-dead Hollywood star at a glance, but her face had given way to his last shot of the back of her head disappearing in the kitchen steam of the Bee Hive.

"Movies," he wrote thinking of his life and her, "are spun out of talking heads. The way the physiological eye prefers light to darkness, the psychological eye selects face over scenery when contained in the same frame." He tucked that note into the drawer with the layers of his random writings. "The camera-work provides the psychology of the movie."

He hoped someday he would start bolt upright in his balcony seat during an *Eyes-and-Ears-of-the-World* newsreel when he would recognize her face modeling clothes in a New York fashion show. Or maybe her face would come back to him as she straddled a horse diving into a tank at Atlantic City. She would surprise him that way and she would be immortal. He was sure she would remember that a living, and more than a living, could be arranged in the movies. She was out there among the stars.

REEL FOUR
Somehow between features he became a teacher.

Time passed. Cinema was everything. He had touched no one and no one had touched him, not counting that warm hand under the dark lavender light of that balcony. In his mind the fear had loomed large that he would live only to thirty, but he was five years overdue and no longer bothering to wonder why he hadn't been taken or why he had not made love. He seemed veined and delicate as a night-blooming orchid. His eyes, which in childhood had been a deep blue, had faded into the uncanny washed-out hue usually found in beach people and ranchers exposed to constant brightness. Light from the silver screen had burned like radiation into his sockets.

Voices told him, advised him, "You can always teach," so for years he taught literature and creative writing. In his lectures, *Leaves of Grass* was a shooting script where Whitman's montage esthetic anticipated Edison's technology; Dickens' editing style generated Eisenstein's; and his punchline for *Ulysses* explained the novel's fluid complexities by revealing that while writing his masterwork, Joyce worked in Dublin as a projectionist. In his writing classes he argued his hippie peacenik students out of turgid undergraduate melodramas about stolen sex and repentant suicide and death in Vietnam. He tutored them into screenplays personal in matter and disciplined in technique. His colleagues regarded him indulgently, urging him over an occasional sherry to invent courses with titles like "Film Interpretation," "Novels into Film," or "Movies and the Liberal Arts." But always he shook his head.

"Why not?" they always asked. "Is the novel any less pleasurable when read as a class assignment?"

Always he smiled pleasantly and excused himself from the hearty company of them and their cheery wives. He was an alien they tried to corral. If he would not invent their courses, then they would have him married, and when married, they would have him father children. Somehow he had given no hostages to fortune; no wife begged him, for the sake of the family food and shelter, to capitulate his secret cinema pleasures to their university schedule. He was a private person and his privacy kept him free. No one could exploit what they did not know. His privacy was, before all, his right.

"Perhaps," one faculty wife whispered, "he abstains from the sexual revolution entirely. There is that rarity called chastity, I believe."

She had glimpsed something of the ideal fire deep in him that gave color to his cheeks.

The wife of his Department Chairman took his arm and pulled him aside. "My husband," she said, "finds you amazingly droll. We're so happy you joined our little group of eccentrics. I mean, that's what teaching is all about, isn't it?"

He watched her tilt her glass to her lips. Her drink was gone but for the ice which stuck for a moment to the bottom of the upturned cylinder. Her braceleted wrist jarred the glass sharply to break the wet freeze. The cold avalanche of cubes slid toward her lips which parted and bit off the advancing ice.

"You know," she said, "you are the still water that runs deep."

So he became water and flowed away from her, in flight from all the pursuers of his life.

REEL FIVE
In mummy movies, every diamond has a curse.

Waiting in the box-office line of the Campus Theater, he worried about himself. He was older, not suddenly, but slowly as in a series of dissolves, conscious that the youth culture, wild in the streets, trusted no one over thirty; but he hardly looked middle-aged, he was sure of it. His hair had thinned a bit, but nothing that some artful combing and men's hairspray wouldn't fix, unless he got caught in a headwind; and the skin around his eyes had wrinkled no more than to a moviegoer's permanent squint. His boyish weight had maintained under the discipline of popcorn, no butter and no salt. He was vainly prideful he had not gotten fat. Perhaps he was, like Monty Clift, one of those neurasthenic cases he had read about.

He no longer climbed up to the balconies. With each paid admission in newer and stranger theaters, he sat closer and closer to the silver screen, not trying to find once again, he told himself, the unseen hand in the lavender light. He sat absolutely alone always staring at the screen, never looking left or right, no matter who came and went in the seats around him. Sometime, he feared, he would walk into a theatre, glide to the front rows, and be sucked up into the screen, lost forever in the 2000-watt glow of the Cinemascope feature presentation. Only his notes, theory on cinema scrawled in the dark, would remain strewn between the seats. No one, not even the janitor, would be curious enough to read them or wonder where the man in the first row had disappeared. He panicked and felt his breath go shallow. He shed his coat and retreated back into the lobby.

The small Campus Theatre was an art house co-featuring foreign films with experimental underground films. The hippie audience was intense, even reverential in the lobby, intoning the names of drugs and directors, congregating around the pot of free coffee. He waited behind a petite young woman who blocked his way to the cups. A wreath of flowers crowned her long blonde hair so straight it looked ironed. She was all bracelets and beads and madras. With her middle finger she dabbed repeatedly at the surface of her steaming cup. He grew impatient. The next feature, Bertolucci's *Last Tango in Paris,* was about to begin. He cleared his throat. He coughed.

"Something's floating in my coffee," she said, turning to him. "Like wax or oil or something."

She was really quite lovely in her motley layers of scarves and beads.

He smiled coolly and placed his own cup in its plastic holder and held it under the tap. He pulled the spigot down and the coffee bubbled black in the cone-bottom of the cup. He teased it to the rim. His hand was steady as he raised the steaming cup to his lips.

"It's wax," she said. "Definitely wax from the cup. It won't hurt you."

He looked at her. He was embarrassed. They seemed to be standing together as much as the other couples in the lobby. Three of his literature students passed by. "Good evening, Professor," one of them said. The other two smiled. He moved away from the woman, who was hardly more than a girl, and nodded to his students over his coffee. She moved with him. He moved again. She followed. They seemed to be dancing in the middle of the lobby. The students pretended not to notice.

"I'm NanSea SunStream. It's a mantra. I'm an Aries. I chant. Enchanted, I'm sure." She extended her hand, reaching for his which he did not offer. She recouped with so gracefully circular a gesture she seemed always to have intended to pull her lustrous blonde hair back behind her ear. "Something tells me you're a Gemini. With a moon in Leo. And, maybe, a Scorpio rising sign."

Music from the screen sounded the Main Title. He turned nervously toward the door, turned back to her, shrugged and smiled and left her standing. He found his way down the aisle to the front. This was his fourth viewing of the movie unreeling on the screen. He knew exactly what would happen from beginning to end and he found comfort in that. Occasionally a film might break or the reels become confused, but overall he enjoyed an order in cinema he did not feel with people. On the screen everything was arranged and directed.

"Here's some sugar," NanSea said, slipping into the seat beside him. "Better take one lump since you half-drank it."

Behind him someone shushed them.

She whispered. "How can you drink that varnish? I couldn't sit back there thinking of you drinking that. I couldn't keep my mind on the film. I've seen it before."

He set his coffee cup on the floor. He knew people like her added lysergic acid to sugar cubes.

"What's that?" She pointed to his notes. "I'll bet you're a movie critic. Wow! I should be quiet so you can concentrate. It's like I understand. I mean, one of the places I hang out is the campus. This is so far out!"

He tried to will her away, but her blonde presence shimmered luminous next to him. Her flawless young face glowed in reflections from the screen. She could have been in the film. He leaned to the opposite arm. He could not help studying her profile that was so like the winsome Gish sisters. She leaned forward, cupped her hand around the lighter she held to a half-smoked joint. "Want a hit?" she asked. He shook his head. "More for me then." She inhaled in short, sharp huffs, and exhaled in measured puffs. He, who had to remember to breathe, envied her even as she relaxed down to perfect silence.

He wished her gone and gathered his notes together. He long ago had ceased bumping into people to discover how it would be with them and he certainly had no recognizable desire to be with her.

"Hey," she said. "You going?"

He was already near the end of the row.

"What would a girl like me," she said loud enough for him to hear, "want with a square like you?"

As he neared the aisle seat, a large old woman sitting in a pile of shopping bags said, "Why don't you two fight at home!"

He escaped to the men's room and locked himself in the middle stall. No one could reach him or see him. He sat and lamented the broken sanctity of even this small neighborhood university theatre. "Somehow," he jotted into his notes, "the shrines are all broken and my Lady Cinema is dead." For a long while he sat, not hearing the door banging open and closed, nor the sound of the urinals flushing. Finally he looked to the stall wall and saw his initials written on an earlier visit. It pleased him that proof remained that he had been there before and saddened him that he would never come there again. He wet his finger and rubbed hard on the ink of his signature. The rubbing made a squeaking sound and caused a shoe in the stall next to his to tap up and down, moving toward him.

He recognized the sexual Morse code. He gasped for air. He pulled himself together and escaped quickly up the stairs, through the lobby, pulling on his coat—Oh, Mr. Coates!—in the middle of the street. He was miles and cities and years away from the arrangements made for him at the Bee Hive and the Apollo and he could only go home for the night.

Behind him, he heard NanSea SunStream calling after him. "Hey! Wait! I didn't mean it. You're cool. You're different. You want to come over for some wine..."

He took a deep breath.

"...some music..."

He walked faster.

"...or something like whatever."

He ran.

REEL SIX
The man who loved movies.

Why he wondered, do people believe that a man who is not married is available to anyone? No one understands vocation anymore. No one accepts dedication. No one believes in chastity.

He sat upstairs in the old house he had bought, locked safely behind the door of a closet large enough to be a small study. Snippets and yards of film footage clipped on fine wires were strung the length of the room: movie millimeters of eight and super-eight and sixteen and thirty-five and wide-screen seventy. The air was acrid with acetone editing glue. Its smell intoxicated him. A twelve-yard sequence of a Technicolor musical- comedy was wrapped around his neck, its ends trailing down his front like a priest's ritual stole. The hot light of his hand-editor had dried the moisture in his nostrils, chapped his lips, and wrinkled his forehead. Its glare threw his shadow huge against the wall-size screen that pulled down over the only door to the hidden room. Nightly he illuminated his celluloid strips the way monks once lovingly tooled manuscripts in lonely cells. He had only to arrange the sequences snipped from this movie and that movie into his own unreeling vision of what a film should be. Life, his waitress had told him was to be had in the movies, so he had waited, waited his whole life, for the return of the unseen hand in the lavender light.

REEL SEVEN
The Transfiguration of the Spieler.

In his own time and by his own decision, he approached his colleagues. He smiled and was almost deferential as he made appointment to lecture in their Departmental Colloquium. Late nights he brooded in the very auditorium where in no time at all his much anticipated talk would be given. As the hour approached, he gathered his reels about him and taxied to the university theater. The seats and aisles and stairs were jammed. Students mixed with faculty. Even people from the local Town-and-Gown society arrived to hear him speak.

When he walked to the podium, the audience hushed expectantly. A slight murmur washed through the balcony and died. He raised his hand. The projectionist dimmed the lights and rolled the silent film.

His movie, ten-years-in-the-editing, was a montage, no, a barrage of hot light, choice sequences, brilliant frames, subliminal images, and remix snippets of found footage he had carefully scratched with pins, streaked with bleach, and hand-colored with multi-hued dyes.

Facing his audience, he stood in the center of the silent screen, looked, in fact, to be part of the screen as the images reflected off his pale skin and white clothing. The audience shifted and whispered in their seats. They expected from him something new, *avant garde*, possibly weird, maybe shocking, and hopefully wonderful. Somewhere an undergraduate girl giggled nervously.

"The silents," he began to speak into his lavaliere mike, "were never silent. Prosperous theatres featured orchestras. Small theatres had pianos and the clack of the projectors. Ethnic theatres hired monologuists to translate the written English titles for the neighborhood. The spielers, as they were called, freely ad-libbed, very freely ad-libbed, many a dull title and plot into gracious wit and good humor. They added dimension to the flat screen."

Only the shadow cast by his body on the screen helped differentiate him among the fast flash of images from Edison, Lumiere, Melies, Lange, Von Sternberg, and Riefenstahl to Brakhage, Anger, Deren, Warhol, Lean, Wilder, Hitchcock, and Bergman.

"In sixty minutes of film," his voice boomed through the theatre, "you actually watch twenty-seven minutes of total darkness. But the mind chooses to see only the remaining thirty-three minutes of light. I want to know what is between those frames, what is in that twenty-seven-minute darkness, what secret of life lies just out of reach in the flickers between those frames."

He began to pelt the audience with data.

"The very form of cinema is absurd. No picture moves. Still frame connects to still frame. The eye cancels the darkness, cancels the stasis. The brain aches for motion. The body aches for life."

He no longer heard the doors of the theatre auditorium opening and closing.

"The first movie audiences in Paris screamed and stampeded as Lumiere's train pounded toward them."

He dropped his arms to his sides and stared up directly into the projector light beaming down hard as grace upon him.

"We each," he said, "make our own movie."

He no longer turned his head. He panned it left and right. He no longer walked toward the stage edge. He tracked. The blink of his eyes became the click of a single frame. He blinked them quickly and the audience became a flicker. His talking became a whirr and his tongue turned to film feeding out of his face.

The gallery of his colleagues and the audience of his students rose to their feet cheering his passion. The applause continued at the reception arranged by his department.

"Very nice," the chairman's wife said, "very nice indeed. You really should develop that film course my husband wants so much. But come," she said, arranging the knot of his tie, "you simply must meet everyone."

CBGB 1977!
(Hunting the Wild Mapplethorpe Model)

The media call it "Punk Rock" and to me *punking* always meant *fucking*. I got my curiosity through the *New York Times* and from hanging out with sickboy Mapplethorpe who was all over his punk diva, that poetic Patti Smith girl who was actually happening. So I figured to check it out. The clubs are a gonzo dream for a New Journalist in search of kink and ink. Editors pay by the column inch for reportage any man would do for free in the underground world of black leather, rock 'n' roll, and sex. Mixed with art and cameras, social devolution is only interesting served raw before it becomes pure style on the runways and in the malls. CBS News got a boner showing a clip of "punk dancing" which to me looked like a lot of fighting, punching, and kick-boxing with a beat. So I split out of Mapplethorpe's loft where I was staying on Bond Street, fucking with him among his cameras and curios, and exited by Bleecker Street and headed to the bottom of the Bowery, stepping over for crissakes winos cadging tourists for bottles of Tawny Port.

Somewhere in the middle of all this lower New York garbage, *Time* tells tourists, and Mapplethorpe tells me, lies CBGB, the hole-in-the-wall capital of Punk Rock. CBGB stands for "Country/Blue Grass/Blues." Shit. Those initials long ago lost their meaning. CBGB is closer now to heeby-jeeby with a gothic-mod crowd that down-shifts the concept of *fabou* to a new low cool. So no wonder Mapplethorpe, Hasselblad in hand, mentioned to keep an eye open for models if I met anyone with a "Look."

Outside CBGB, a Bowery drunk and his three pals were tossing up cookies in the doorway. (Hey, man, New Journalism reportage *is* what it is *about*! And punk is about the Stuff of the Night. Fluids. Sex. Blood. Art. And other outrageous dark voodoo that scares Mom and Pop like the inside of CBGB). I stumbled in through the gloom over loose floorboards, tripping on gigantic roaches, and plopped my ass into a wobbly chair made in a correctional facility for terminal assholes, trying to see the goddam stage. Outside, the Bowery Bum Ballet had sounded like all four faces on Mount Retchmore doing an upchuck quartet. Inside, CBGB was stirring like a morgue of necrophiliacs anticipating a hot autopsy.

Tonight. On stage. Live. Sort of. Was appearing the punk rock group, SMEGMA 4SKINZ.

Looking around, I saw weirdos. I mean young, young, young weirdos. Before hippies, people didn't get weird till maybe twenty-five or thirty. These babies were born weird. All of them, not old enough to grow a moustache, looked cloned out of what was left of James Dean. They had deadwhite faces made up over black leather jackets.

Fuck. Gimme an empty table. Quick.

To my right sat Fan Tan Fanny. One fan came out of her crotch and spread out over her tiny chest. The second fan came out of her ass and reached up and across her pale shoulders where the two fans joined, baring her mortuary sides. Her small dead breasts dangled forward as she leaned to light her Camel from the table candle.

She was no apprentice nymphomaniac.

The guy behind me was no guy to have behind me. He was a burnt-out twenty-two, 6'2", and 300 of the ugliest pounds this side of a fat man's amputated left leg. His tit-length beard, parted in the middle, spread out to two sticky points. His shaved head was covered with Day-Glo green bristle. His tits, his nose, and his left ear were pierced. The lobe stretched, like something out of *National Geographic*, halfway down his neck. Through the hole in his lobe he had stuck a big, corked test tube. Inside the test tube crawled two live cockroaches.

Suddenly the stage was lit. The houselights dimmed to black. A deafening hum buzzed feedback from the speakers on either side of the floor. A disembodied voice announced, "Ladies and Gentlemen! SMEGMA 4SKINZ!"

As the stage lights blazed bright, then down, something dark pulled up a chair to my table. In the candlelight, I saw he was young and leathered. Our eyes met. Some fucking enchanted evening. His face had the tough hollow look Jim Morrison had perfected in that bathtub in Paris. He took out a Gauloises Blondes. I struck a match. He moved his face to the flame. The cigarette dangled. He inhaled and sort of grunted thanks. I dropped the lit match into his leather crotch. Our thighs touched side-by-side under the table. He smiled and licked his lips. He sucked on a cut across his knuckles. "I punched a guy," he said. He held out his bloody fingers. "Want a taste?"

"SMEGMA sucks," I said.

"Mr. Gauloises" smiled and snorted his agreement. I checked him out again. He looked at me as if he were asking for something I knew I had.

The music was too loud to make normal conversation.

On stage, Pontius and Pilate, the leaders of SMEGMA 4SKINZ, were laying out their opening number. Pontius Smegma wore a blue ski jacket and stretch pants. He stood stage-rear moving his hands without any particular effect up and down on a synthesizer. He made elevator Muzak sound like the Pachelbel "Canon in D." Pilate Smegma's leather jacket was torn to shreds. How the fuck can anyone tear up a leather jacket? His black Korvette's $1.98 wig slipped to his stencilled eyebrows as he struggled to look EVIL.

"Sixty-nine Cumshots!" Pilate Smegma shouted, then hit himself in the side of the face with the microphone torn from its stand. POW! "Sixty-nine Cumshots! SIXTY-NINE CUMSHOTS!" He screamed. Then POW! POW! POW! Slamming himself in the side of the face.

"WHAT'S YOUR NAME?" I yelled into Mr. Gauloises' ear.

"You can call me 'Bryl.'"

Behind his nose ring, he looked like his parents called him "Buddy."

I pretended not to hear him and leaned over for another listen using his right thigh to support my weight.

I pressed hard. Very hard. "Did you say 'Bryl'?" I asked.

"Yeah," he said "A little dab'll do ya. Brylcreme. But nobody ever calls me 'Mr. Creme.'"

Crissakes. This kid was straight out of the Toob.

The music was maxing. The crowd was rushing the stage for a taste of SMEGMA. The bleeding performer was alternating his mike from his mouth to his asshole, jamming it for a few hot licks into the faces worshipping him. Before he could sing another chorus of "I Wanna Eat Your Load," I asked Bryl, "You want to go out for a good smoke?"

We shouldered our way to the door. A Testosterone Case with Popeye forearms stamped our hands as we left. Stepping over the bum and his pals lying in their puke-o-rama, we headed into the alley behind the club. It smelled of piss. We ignored the skag servicing the suit.

"Okay, Mr. Creme. What's your real story?"

He looked at me like a naughty cocker spaniel who just shit on the rug and expected the Sunday *Times* across his ass. I reached for his leather lapels. His right hand shot up and grabbed mine. The back of his hand was angry, red, and blistered with fresh cigarette burns.

Terrific. Another creature from Alpha Centauri.

I shook his hand away and slapped him across the face. He went down like shot snot. He knelt in the bum piss and clutched my knees like the Saving Cross and whimpered. I grabbed the shoulder of his jacket, un-snapped the epaulets and using them as handles, forced the punkfucker's shoulders back up against the wall. He grabbed my foot and put the sole of my boot square against his chest. Lordy! Make me a footstool at thy feet! Taking his cue, I crushed him against the wall. His tongue stuck out wet and sticky licking the toe of my boot.

For something in his youth or childhood, he deserved, or thought he deserved, the kind of thing I got to give. I could see a bulge rising in his tight Levi's. My own cock was at fighting stance. (What do authorities mean about sex *and* violence. Sex *is* violence. These days.) Outpunking this punk was not a problem. He reached for his fly held closed by six big safety pins. I scraped my boot down, knocking his hand away.

"Mine," I said. "Me. Me. Me. Mine. Asshole!"

With trembling hands he reached up and unlatched my Harley belt. Slowly he popped open my buttons. He lowered my jeans to my knees. Who the fuck wears underwear? My cock sprang out toward his face. I was gonna have me my first genuine certified punk mouth. I slapped him once more, just for the bloody good juice of it. "Not so fast." I spit on him. When in Punkdom, do as the punks do. "We got all night. Go slow. Treat it nice."

Bryl reinvented the blowjob. He had an all-pro tongue. Every few seconds he raised his mournful eyes to check if he was licking me all right. I sneered my best Presley sneer-of-death. Elvis would have liked my version of his style.

Gradually, Bryl worked his way to my roots. He sucked long and steady. I was almost this side of cuming when suddenly goddam coughing came from my left. The soylent green bums had found their way into the alley for more puke time in the old corral. I pulled up my jeans. "Later," I said.

We showed our stamped hands to Mr. Testosterone at the CBGB door. SMEGMA had finished trying and a new group was on stage. A table opened up. We sat thigh to thigh.

"Hey, Fuckers! Meet PLUGG AND THE DRAIN BOYS!"

The crowd managed a cheer. Yay. Yay. Who the fuck are THE DRAIN BOYS? They looked like abortions that got away. The guitar-punk wore a tight dog collar. A safety pin dangled from his ear. The lead singer, Plugg, was meditating, masturbating, waiting his cue, stripped to the waist, ropes of drool hanging from his mouth to his muscular belly. Suddenly he sprang to his dead feet and started the song: "Why do I wanna fuck you Girls when your dog is so mean Girls I don't wanna hold your gland Girls I'm talkin about a plan Girls I don't really want you Girls I need sex Yeah Baby I NEED SEX!" (This shit is copyright 1977 by Plugg Drain Music.)

Bryl and I looked at each other. *Suddenly*, because everything happens *suddenly* in the punk world, Plugg threw himself from the stage into the audience, landing on our table. Our two bottles of beer crashed to the floor. We kicked him the shit away just for the fuck of it and he crawled back onto the stage toward the drums. He stuck his head inside the bass drum to really hear a few hot beats then threw himself onto the floor again, flopping like the beached fish at the end of Fellini's *La Dolce Vita*.

Again, *suddenly*, another punk from the audience dashed for the stage. Just as *suddenly* the vicious-looking DRAIN BOYS drummer rose from behind his drums, and with his sticks in his thick mitts played twelve bars of "Bolero" on the punk's face. The entire CBGB broke into a mass of flailing fists and screams. The punk, who now knew "Bolero" by heart, was hum-wiping his bleeding face across the safety-pinned tits of a tattooed earth-mother punkette. Fan Tan Fanny ran trailing her rear fan along the floor. Behind us, glass shattered.

"You want to blow this joint?" I asked.

"What?"

"Are you ready for your close-up?"

I pulled Bryl to the door.

"Wait a minute," he said. Outside, he dropped his jeans, squatted, parted his cheeks, grunted twice, and dumped a load on the heeby-jeeby sidewalk. Street light showed off bone structure and boner and butt.

We walked east through the meanest part of the Village. Bryl's punk-patrol attitude made anyone we passed choose to think we were invisible. We reached the East River. No problem. I turned to Bryl. "Okay," I said. "Now where were we? Oh yeah. Now your little dab'll do me. Do me!"

He stood mute.

I punched him in the stomach as hard as I could. He turned green. I could see that puke-look a guy gets in his crossed eyes, so I grabbed him by his greasy hair and held his head over the water in the dark river below. Why the fuck mess up one more nice city sidewalk? He up-chucked straight beer. This kid was gonna end up back in the Bowery, but right now he was in bloom and hot. "You and the night and the sewage," I said. He sank to his knees, lapping at my crotch like the East River lapped at the cement wall below us. God! I felt poetic. I also felt hard again. "Stop!" I said.

He looked up at me, his mouth still around my cock like a punk choirboy caught on the fourth note of "O Holy Night." I slapped him hard and he let go. "Turn around,"

I said.

He opened his mouth to speak. I raised my hand. He obeyed. "Drop your jeans."

He reached for his belt and dropped his trousers. "Now, boy, down like a dog." He went down on all fours.

"Bryl," I said, "they should call you 'Doggy.'" I steered my cock straight toward his asshole. Was he ready? Is Flushing in New York? I plunged in. Surprise. He was tighter than I expected. Good. New punk. I pumped him harder. Car lights flashed by. His butthole bloomed. New York rose bright all around us in the dark. His ass had talent a camera would love. His mouth was chanting fuck-me-fuck-me. I pulled out. He thought I was finished. He had another thought to think. I pushed him down further. "Okay, Bryl baby, daddy's gonna teach his doggie a new trick."

A shiver ran down his spine. He wagged his butt. Somewhere in the summer night conga music floated on the fucka-fucka air.

I rubbed my hand through the thick Brylcreme in his hair, then held it at his mouth. "Slobber on it," I said.

Without question he slurped my hand. The mix of beerpuke, saliva, and punk grease lubed my fist just fine.

He whined "I can't take that." He nursed a small brown bottle of poppers.

"Don't play Brer Rabbit with me." I pushed my middle finger into his asshole. "Easy," I said. "You're easy." I slipped in my ring finger. "Greasy." Then my index finger. "Sleazy." He moaned. I reached under with my other hand and pulled his butt back to me by his balls. He had a safety pin stuck through his cock. Sirens screamed over the rumble of traffic. My pinky slipped in. "Cheesy."

His butthole snapped at my knuckles. I bent my thumb across my palm and drove my fist home to the wrist. The suction of his butt pulled my arm in deeper. I braced my boots.

"What you on?" I said.

He made whining sobs. Music to my ears.

"You underestimate yourself," I said. "Big punks don't cry."

He whined again, but his butt suctioned like a sump and my fist turned a slow 180 to the right and a faster 180 left. Oh yeah. I punchfucked him loose. He liked it. I withdrew my fist and stroked my hard cock, listening to him pleading fuck-me-fuck-me. The night was hot. I spit on my dick and wrapped my fist around it. His butt pucker made little kiss-kiss-kissy sounds flirting with my cock. Like a hand grenade, I jammed my fist, full of my dick, into the ventriloquist lips of his butt. His fruit juicy young hole was punk perfect. His internal heartbeat pulsated around my forearm. I humped away, moving my fist inside his asshole jerking off my dick inside my fist inside his butt. Hell, I even let the guy jerk at himself. And, oh God, how he pulled, his ass-ring tightening down harder on my fist and cock till *suddenly* we both *suddenly* shot off *suddenly* together arching up in shouts and juice and rapture into the noise and light of the brilliant New York night that left CBGB down below like a dot on a grid.

God bless participatory journalism.

I kicked him down on the sidewalk. "You been fist-fucked, punk."

"It hurt."

"What's your point?"

"I liked it."

"No shit!"

He licked my greasy hand and looked up at me. "You want to go back to CBGB?"

"Fuck that noise."

We cleaned up with a rubber hose at a faucet outside a warehouse. In the lamplight, I figured next day I'd take Bryl back to meet Mapplethorpe at his studio.

"You ever modeled for a photograph?" I asked.

"I can't show my face."

"It ain't about your face, Fist Boy."

On our way back to the West Village, we saw two girls on a stoop. When we passed, they looked up. One of them pointed.

"Mira, Juanita, mira!" she said. "Los punks! Los punks!"

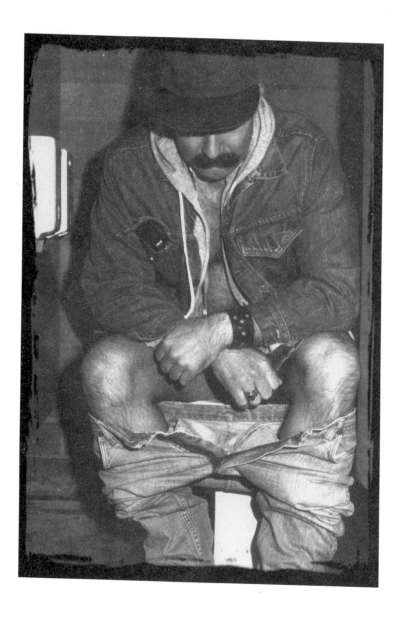

WORSHIP ME!

Joint in his mouth, he sat on the toilet with the stall door as wide open as his thighs. He was so hot he was cool. It was the summer of '72, and Market Street was all torn up for the new BART subway, which is where this guy had climbed from at the end of a hard day digging, setting his bare butt down on the black horseshoe topping the porcelain commode. More than one subway groundhog found his way up the busy backstairs of the Embarcadero YMCA. Those days, cruising knew no labels.

Anyway, his hand was down between his big thighs, massaging his meat. Hearing the splashing, I figured he was wetting the head of it in the toilet water. Nice and sleazy. He was Italian, maybe 27, rugged, good-sized arms in his filthy white teeshirt. He had long sideburns and a moustache and medium-long hair curling up around his yellow construction helmet that said JOE in handwriting like you usually only see in graffiti. He looked at me and spit on the tile floor. I spit too. We wore almost identical jeans, boots, and shirt. He snorted a fuck-you-asshole laugh, curled his lip, and nodded me in closer. He took a big hit off his joint and exhaled a flume of blue smoke into my mouth and pushed me back, grinning, sharing dope he knew I didn't need.

He took his big wet hand off his tool. His cock itself boinged up, dripping toilet water. The look in his eye was mean and nasty. His dick was enormous. Thick at the base, rooted in black curlicues of coarse Italian hair, his meat stuck up, I'll be honest, at least nine inches, and maybe ten. I wanted his frosting-white gelato. I could tell he was hot to feed me.

I fell to my willing knees between what I still remember as the best pair of authentic construction-worker thighs that ever squeezed me into submission to suck his big cock. He grabbed my ears and slammed my face into his crotch, impaling my mouth on his shaft, burying himself, so I could memorize the full feel of his doubledip cockhead down behind my Adam's apple. I'm a born sucker of big cocks, especially when they're attached to a man of some power and authority who wants one thing and one thing only: to get himself crazy while he facefucks his dick, in no fucking hurry to get his nut, taking his sweet time to play, turning on every square inch of his shaft and head.

I remember he said, "You like it, huh? It big enough for you, huh? A choker, ain't it? Gag on it, cocksucker."

His dick answered his questions for me. He drove his rod like a tape-measure into me as far as it would go. I looked up at him, and he was this powerful young tough guy, like he was some dialog-balloon fantasy coming hookah-tookah out of my mouth like Acapulco-Gold smoke. (He had me buzzed.) But he was real, right down to his dripping armpits and gold wedding band and gold cross tangled in the hair on his chest. His forearms and biceps were muscular. He used them to hand-drive my head down on his cock. He liked the power of sitting on the porcelain throne with me kneeling between his thighs from which there was no-escape possible or wanted.

"I'm drillin' you, shithead. I'm fuckin' drillin' you with my big rig." He roughfucked my throat, searching for my gag-reflex. With his dick so big and his action so rough, he found it fast. Lucky he stayed seated, because I lost my top tray of cookies, and he laughed like a groundhog sure of his tunneling.

I was on my knees, willingly. This was no late-show SM scene. The style was all his, probably the same his wife got, when he got her, while he was no doubt thinking about something else. Guys with big cocks aren't like other guys. They're different from the rest of us. They got more, so they want more, and they figure they got more coming to them; and all of us act like they do, because we know they do, because we like to swing on big, beautiful, hard-sculpted male cocks, and because a man with a big cock deserves special treatment—he just does. My daddy told me so.

"Asshole," he said. "Lick your slop off my family fuckin' jewels." His balls were big, low-hangers, as noble as his cock. I bet the fucker sired a rugrat every nine months unless he was filling up rubbers real juicy every night and tossing them at pictures of the pope. "You want my load," he said. "You're gonna suck my seed like my dick's the longest, thickest, fattest straw you ever sucked on."

Oh Lawdy, Mizz Clawdy! When some men late at

night act out lines like that, I laugh, unless they're hung over ten inches and then I don't care what they say; but this guy was fucking r-e-a-l! How often is the actual man sitting on a YMCA toilet, with his shirt stripped off, his thighs spread, his big dirty construction boots wrapped around your waist, and his dick jutting ten inches straight up his Italian belly, also your fantasy come true?

Life being what it is. Not often.

So when he ordered me to stay put kneeling, I did, even when he leaned forward, stuck two greasy-nailed, tobacco-stained fingers in my mouth, and belched and farted at the same time. He made life real simple. He shit-kicked through life with an open fly. He stood up on the black horseshoe toilet seat like it was a dais and he was a dago statue. "Lick 'em," he said, meaning his dirty boots, which I did, desperate to earn his big cock back in my mouth. My own dick was hard and desperate as Butch Cassidy in the last reel.

Standing on the seat, he towered over me kneeling on the floor. He was a specimen. His All-American beauty translated perfectly from the Italian. He spit down on me. I opened my mouth. He spit again. Bulls-eye! Two points! I swallowed the hawker. His cock rose like a missile from a silo.

"Worship me," he said.

The toilet stall exploded with a dago Day-Glo mix of paganism and Catholicism strong enough to scandalize the Young Men's Christian Association.

"Worship me."

"I worship you." I said it. I meant it.

"Worship me!"

He wrapped his right hand tight around the base

of his dick, the head grew purple, monstrous. "Worship my big cock! Worship my huge fucking dago dick!"

I rose licking up his hairy inner thighs. His hand beat his rod. I rose past his bobbling balls. My nose and mouth and eyes rose directly below his fist slamming his dick. Accidentally? On purpose? Who knows? Who cares? His masturbating fist bloodied my nose.

"I worship your big fucking prick," I said and sucked blood.

His curly head reared back. His daywork-dirty body contracted. Muscles started popping out. Then veins. Saving his right hand for his dick, he grabbed my hair with his left, and, inch by fast inch by faster inch, drove his throbbing, cuming cock, convulsing, shooting, deep into my mouth, drilling me with his big rig, driving his rod, cubic inch by linear inch, down my throat, plowing the inner route toward my asshole like I was some goddam subway tunnel he was gonna ream out or else.

If my life, or his, ever gets made into a porno movie, this part absolutely must be slow-motion, because, as the Village People are my witness, every inch is true.

SEDUCING BUTCH:
TATTOOED ARYAN BIKER

Dear Dr. Strangelove: I like seducing straight guys. Not that straight is better than gay, mind you, just less accessible, and so more of a challenge. To make a short story short, last Christmas I took my lover's mother to, where else, the Mall, and, of course, after feeling up every piece of merch in six stores, she had to go to the Powder Room, which, in Malls, is always hidden off somewhere behind the shops, like they're pretending no one in Malls ever pees.

You should have seen the trailer talent in the hall outside the room where the chorus line was waiting to powder. Ten deep. What is it with the capacity of women's toilets? Even Santa Claus had a shorter line. Every other girl and her two baggy-clothes friends had a baby stroller. My lover's mother joined the waiting crew. I checked my watch.

Every curse has a blessing. Leaning up against the hall wall like he belonged there was this 5-8, 160# chunk of biker in a black leather jacket with red stripes down the outside of his arms. He was no more than 24 with a blond moustache and a wispy beard. His jeans were clean, but you could see where even Tide couldn't wash out the grease. He'd rolled them up twice in cuffs exposing the kind of slouch-broken boots you'd like to put between two pieces of Wonderbread for lunch.

Was he waiting for his woman? Or was he just lurking outside the men's toilet? He looked the doper kind of straight that you figure if the time is right, you can score. I cruised by him like a ship passing doo-be-doo-be-doo in the night. He kept his posture, hips, and basket thrust forward, like he was staring into mid-distance for ET to come home to blow him. Fine with me. I got a close shot of his dick in the tight bulge of his crotch. Fine, fine meat. Not bad potatoes either. Okay. So I went and whizzed. When I came out, his trailer nymph was standing next to him. Have you ever noticed how guys-who-are-so-hot-you-could-die always have a case of terminal cellulite in tow eating a giant bag of potato chips? I guess in America lower-class fellas are never told how universally handsome they are when they're in bloom for the only six months of their lives they'll ever be in bloom. The thought never crosses their mind.

It crossed mine. So the dude walks off into the Mall with his babe in search of more fast food venues, and I wait for my mother-in-law to piddle and return. That night, when my lover, whom I really love, made love, my mind was full of the hot young biker I'd never see again.

But, wait! Three days later, driving my lover's mother in my red Ford F-100 pickup to catch the Airporter to

SFO, who should I see, but the same guy walking along the shoulder of the road. I hit the gas, jumped the speedbumps at the hotel, threw out the mother-in-law's bag, and the mother-in-law, and told her, normally I'd wait till the Airporter bus left, but something had come up. Like lust. We kiss-kissed good-bye, and I peeled out of the lot and down the road hoping Lust was still walking in the same direction.

He was. I pulled over a 100 feet ahead of him and watched his approach in both my rearview and side mirror. He came right by my open window, and said, "How ya doin', bud?" There *is* a gay God. There is a *gay* God. There is a gay *God*. So, anyway, I laid this line on him how I was a video photographer and I'd like to shoot him, "And, of course, I'll pay you."

"When?" he said.

"How about now."

"Sounds good to me." He climbed in. Not one word was spoken about sex the whole way to my driveway, not even when we got into the house, not even when I turned on the video lights, not even when I got down behind the video camera. I figured even if I couldn't have him physically, I could jerk off to him electronically on my 40-inch screen where he'd be almost life-size, or better, in close-up.

So I started to ask him questions to shift his southern-drawl voice into full "you-all." Well, let me truly confess, guys like him love to talk about themselves. After twenty minutes of his studly bullshit about his downtime in the slammer, I asked him about the tattoos on his arms and did he have any on his chest and belly, and, "Why don't you just pull off your shirt so I can video them while you tell me how you got them." These guys are always vain about their tats. He stripped off the shirt revealing the jailhouse tattoos on his nice chest with one ornate script *FTW* (Fuck The World) on his right pec above the ship on his cute little beer belly. His big basket was still bulging in his jeans. That was the next objective.

"So what do you do?" he asked.

Here was my big chance. "I write for straight porn mags."

"Like Larry Flynt?"

"You want to see some?" I doubted he could read much. I just wanted him to look at the pictures of naughty ladies. So I got the mags, and with the camera running, we talked, and then he sort of stopped talking and kept turning pages. Zero hour. Do or die. Kneeling behind the running camera, I gritted my teeth and said, "Why don't you take down your pants." I figured if he said "No" on tape, I could get off on his straightboy attitude.

But, no shit, he stood up, and stripped down. No underwear. Just a clear view of his nice furry balls and his upstanding hardon. A good 7 or 8 inches. Still no mention of sex. I shot him, hardon, turning pages for about five minutes. Then I figured it was time to dare again to push the scene. "It's okay to jerkoff." Permission with excons is part of the program. His hand dropped immediately to his cock. His passion grew. He sprawled on the couch with one hand beating his meat and the other turning pages.

"It's okay to shoot when you want to," I said, hoping he'd take his time, but, no, he was ready, and in two minutes flat, he shot his load straight at my camera. A big load. Juiced all over his cock. He regained his composure.

"Can I wash up?" he said immediately, the way stray young husbands always do.

While he was in the bathroom, I put a straight porno film on the VCR to greet him on his return. He liked that.

"You're gonna make me go again," he said.

Exactly what I had in mind. I laid on the floor with the top of my head touching the base of the 40-inch screen. "Kneel across my chest," I said. He did. His cock and balls were at my chin. His muscular, tattooed torso rose above my face exactly the way I liked in the power-position I directed. "You just go ahead, watch video, and jerkoff while I look up at you and rub your chest and belly and balls."

"You want to cum too? That's cool." (I think he'd done this before.)

And so I did, rubbing him, smelling him, all the while he never looked at me, but kept his straight eyes glued straight on the straight screen, pumping his straight meat, until, finally, when I saw he was ready to cum again, I timed my own hand and dick to cum in the same blast.

Was it wrong, Dr. Strangelove, or was it just desserts, that I kind of liked turning him into a sex object while he was jerking off to women on screen?

I had him for one afternoon. I've got the videotape forever which proves that if you want something enough, and can figure how to work it, you'll make possible what at first seemed impossible.

Otherwise gay guys wouldn't be more clever than straight guys, and we wouldn't be covered with their cum.

She was a Transverse Venus
rising from the Transerotic sea...
Her body the cove of pleasure
for many men...
She was the girl of our
ultimate wet dreams!

I MARRIED AN AQUA-NYMPH

"Wet dreams?" she asked. "All dreams should be wet dreams." She sat perched up in a golden King Neptune chair. She knew how to turn even the jaded Hollywood reporters and photographers on. They threw questions to her. She puckered her red lips. She smiled. Flash cameras dazzled the crowd gathered around the curvy blonde with her luscious legs tucked tight down into her form-fitting mermaid tail. A national poll of adult theater-goers had picked her as the Erotic Star of 1979.

"What's your sign?" The question came from a severely tailored young PoCo Amazon from one of the politically correct sex lib magazines.

"Pisces with an Aquarius moon," she said, patting her green-scaled hips.

"Don't you think your image hardly helps the women's movement?" the Amazon asked, pursing her lipstick lips.

"It's not the women's movement I'm trying to help get hard," she said. Her voice sounded like Mae West and Bette Midler mixed in a tuna can. "I just wanna see men's movement. Ya know what I mean?" She did a one-two take on the sapphic Amazon. "Ya don't know what I mean," she said.

The reporters roared with laughter. Flash guns shot off.

"Honey," she said, "let me explain the facts. Hollywood movies showcase men. Adult films survive on one thing only: great roles for great women."

The Amazon flipped her shorthand pad closed and steamed past me for the exit. Suddenly, she stopped at the door and turned to shout, "You're nothing but an X-rated Esther Williams!" Then she sped through the exit. I myself never was much for movements of any kind that didn't have a sense of humor about themselves. I guess that's why so many men loved Stella Maris: she was born, a pun of nature, with a sense of humor about herself.

"Stella Maris," she said. "That's my real name." She was chewing two sticks of Juicy Fruit. I could smell her sweet hot breath across my desk. "I'm Italian. Sort of. Stella Maris means something in Italian like Star of the Sea. I saw it on a church once. Right on the cornerstone it said my name, Stella Maris Church. I think that's nice, don't you?"

I stared at this looker over my typewriter. I see dozens of girls every day who ask me my opinion about something, about anything, about themselves. There's no girl on earth more eager to please than a girl who wants to make it in Hollywood. Most of them are just pretty enough to get felt up by a few agents and, if they're lucky, fucked by a couple producers and, if they're real lucky, cast in a nonspeaking part as an extra in a TV pilot. By the time they get some screen time, they're usually going down for the third time hooked on sex, drugs, or their own vanity. Every once in a while I recognize a face on screen for a few seconds and then I never see her again. Now you know how far a blow job can get a girl. And how much farther a fuck.

Lots of aspiring young girls are good sex; but that's not what makes a star. A star is a good fuck with that something extra. Stella Maris had it. I knew it from the minute she walked into my office wanting me to write up a phony PR release for her portfolio of glossy pictures.

"I don't have much experience," she said. "I mean I've never really taken acting lessons. Except for when I'm playing out fantasies at home alone, or..." Her voice trailed off. She stopped chewing her gum.

She was beautiful. Tall. Lean. Graceful. Golden touchable skin. She looked like a Venus rising from the sea. A whole new 10!

"Or...what?" I asked.

Her hand played with the small beads of sweat rising on the tan cleavage between her perfectly shaped tits.

"...or when I'm with other guys. Is that okay to say that? I mean, I guess it will have to be. I don't want to be in great big Hollywood movies. I've always fantasized about being in X-rated movies. Do you think that's normal for an All-American girl to want to be a porn star?"

"Honey, every woman in the USA would like to be a porn star."

"But I want to be a big porn star. Bigger than Lovelace or Chambers. I want to make classic erotic films bigger and better than *Deep Throat* and *Behind the Green Door*."

"That's a tall order," I said. "First of all, the competition will eat you up no matter how gorgeous you are or how sexually talented. Second of all, the camera's got to love you, and you've got to make love to the camera. Third, you got to have a gimmick."

She looked at me like I was some kind of shmuck. "I'm the gimmick," she said. She handed me her portfolio. Threw it on my desk. "There," she said. "Open that up and look and see how the camera and I get along! There must be ten pictures there any guy with balls could get off on!"

A handful of glossy pix slipped out of her portfolio onto my cluttered desktop. Some of them were expertly shot. Others looked muddy. Like they had been shot by a friend with a darkroom. No matter. Throughout the whole range of camera-work a certain something about Stella Maris rang true. She had created herself her way.

"Who shot these?" I asked.

"Several men."

"What kind of men?"

"Men I know," she said. She rubbed her index finger lightly around her wet lips. She looked directly at me. Her other hand toyed with a gold amulet hanging on a golden chain around her neck. She wore the sign of Pisces dangling seductively in the cleavage between her incredible tits. Fuck! Guys could fall for this fish—hook, line, and sinker! "They were all shot by men I know. By men who hired me. For pictures. I mean I didn't have sex with them. Well, not with all of them. Just the ones who figured out how to turn me, you know, a little bit crazy. I just want you to know that I have a special talent. And I needed the pictures, just like I need you to write up a public relations piece. Or two. Okay? I mean, I had to trade some of those guys, and a doctor or two, a little bit of what I do best for a little bit of what they do best. Just think of it. Maybe we can make the same kind of deal. What do you think? How about it? Partners?"

"At least," I said, "you're not taxable." I knew times were hard with recession, but to see a girl as gorgeous as Stella Maris bartering her way into a business deal proved that inflation makes strange bedfellows.

"Partners?" she asked again.

"Partners," I said with some hesitation. "We'll see."

"You don't want to ball me?" Stella sounded surprised and a little bit hurt.

"Of course. Of course I want to ball you," I said. But in my thoughts, considerations of her potential as an on-screen fuckable commodity were winning the race with my interested dick. I try never to fuck with my clients. It's a bad idea to get your meat where you earn your bread. "Of course. Any man in his right mind would want to ball you."

"Thanks," she said. She smiled and pulled the Juicy Fruit out of her mouth and rolled it up in a gum wrapper. "Then you'll do it?" she asked.

"Ball you or write your press release?"

"Both," she teased. "In whatever order you want."

"Don't you want the PR copy written first?"

"I trust men," she said.

"You're going to be very popular in Hollywood."

"And I trust you especially," she said.

"Why's that?"

"I don't know. I'm a creature of instinct. I follow my instincts. Always. I'm never wrong. At least hardly ever. I was wrong about a couple lifeguards in Santa Monica. But that was three months ago when I lived over by the ocean. Right after I first arrived in California. I was just nineteen then. Now I'm twenty. I've been around some. I know what I want. I know how I want to get it. And my instincts tell me to trust you." She smiled and reached into her handbag. "This is for you," she said." It's a kind of retainer fee."

"It's a key," I said.

"To my house," she said. She stood up to go.

"Your apartment?"

"I told you I trust you." She smiled and turned her fanny to go out the door. She stopped. "I told you. I act on instinct. You'll see." She blew me a kiss. Just like later on I'd get used to seeing her blow kisses to an admiring press and public. "Bye...."

And she was gone, leaving me stunned in her wake.

What could I have said to her? She trusted me. I couldn't take too much advantage of a woman's trust. Could I? No. I couldn't. I had to pace around my office. The portfolio Stella left with me was too hot to put down. Inside the sealskin folder were more pictures of her in various wet poses as well as a collection of writings from her diary.

Dear Diary:

For the first time I confess on the written page that one of my earliest dreams as a young girl came repeatedly after one summer when all us kids played Tom Sawyer and Becky Thatcher down by the big old creek that ran through the fields just outside our town. I woke up one night in a cold and clammy sweat. I felt all wet between my legs. Water had beaded up on my forehead.

What had I been dreaming? I could feel the dream. All the boys in the neighborhood put their heads together. They decided to kidnap me and take me out on their raft in the creek. I felt them carrying me across the open field. I felt their hands feeling up my body. I felt like a fish out of water. I wanted to get away. But they were stronger than me. They carried me out onto their raft. One of them, the biggest boy of all, stuck his pole in the water and pushed us all off from shore. Another boy unzipped his pants and peed over the side of the raft. His water made little fizzy bubbles in the surface of the creek.

In the middle of the stream, the boys stopped the raft and dropped the rusty old bucket filled with cement that they used for an anchor. I knew what they were going to do. I had heard that they had a clubhouse, like Atlantis, under the creek. This was a dream. Remember. Anything is possible, and permitted, in a dream. They lowered me over the side of the raft. I felt the warm air on my skin turn to the cool chill of the water as the surface of the creek rose slowly up around my feet and ankles, past my knees, and up the inside of my warm thighs. When the shock of the cold water lapped at my little pussy, I think I felt the sweet warm sensation of cuming for the first time. Their hands touched me here and there as they lowered me deeper into the creek. The ring of cold water rose up over my buttocks, up my back and around my belly. My little tits floated for an instant on the cold surface. I felt my nipples harden for the first time. The water rose higher around my throat. My chin bobbed on the surface. I gasped for what I thought was my last breath. The water rose up over my face. My hair floated like a mass of seaweed on the surface.

I felt their hands lowering me give way to hands pulling me down deeper by my feet. I was surprised that other boys had dived off the raft and were reeling me into their underwater lair. I was more surprised when I realized that I could breathe underwater. Breathe better, in fact, than I ever could breathe on land. Air, I suddenly thought, had seemed so thin to me. I found all the oxygen I needed came into me through the water. I opened my eyes. The world under the creek was beautiful.

The boys made me cry, until I discovered they only wanted to make me happy. They kept me in a special room, built out of net, in the center of their underwater hideaway. They kept me naked with the nets draped all around me. The only time they bothered me was when they wanted to play with me. And that made me feel so good that I learned very quickly to lie back in the nets with my legs spread nicely apart. I knew they liked to watch me lying there with one hand on my freshwater pussy and one hand on my breasts.

Everything was so innocent. Everything was so right. I did everything those boys wanted. And after I did it, I wanted to do it all again. With all of them. I guess I must be some kind of throwback or something, to the times when humans lived in the sea. I must be some kind of descendent of the Mermaids. At least that's nice to think.

And think about it I did. This girl didn't need a publicity folder. She needed a keeper. Or so at least I thought at first. Then I began to realize what a wonder she was. The more I read of her diary, the more I understood about this girl whose main turn-on was anything wet and wild! I wanted to keep contact with her; so I called her on the phone. She asked me to drive over to her place in Nichols Canyon the next afternoon. I told her I had a draft of her PR story ready for her approval. Actually, I felt I could write nothing about her until I got more of the mystery of her underwater life-style cleared up. For that reason I arrived up in Nichols Canyon about an hour earlier than she had mentioned. I parked down the road and walked up through the bushes that surrounded her sunswept swimming pool.

Now I'm no more of a Peeping Tom than the next guy. But what I saw going on in that shell-shaped pool made me stand stock-still in the shade of the shrubbery. The pool was sun splashing blue. A small tape cassette wired to large poolside speakers was playing the haunting love-sounds of dolphins courting. I got hornier than the dolphins themselves. Because there was Stella, naked as a fish, floating on her serene back in the pool. Her luxurious hair floated like a crown around her head. Her tits poked up above the surface of the water. Her nipples were beaded around the aureole with crystal droplets of water. Her crotch rose and fell with the tidal lap of the pool licking up at her golden pussy. Her eyes were closed. A smile rested on her face.

She was the perfect female laid back deep into the wet reaches of her turn-on. She broke her smile only occasionally. Just enough to match the cooing, blowing sounds of the male dolphins wailing on the tape. She never opened her eyes.

I rose up to watch her more closely over the privet

hedge and fence. This girl Stella could rattle a guy's cage. If I had any doubts about her X-rated star quality, this keyhole peep show in daylight brighter than the lights on any movie set dispelled them.

Watching the long lissome tanned golden body of Stella Maris floating in the warm wet of her Southern California pool convinced me to do anything and everything I could to help this ambitious and offbeat girl become a major erotic film star.

I found out right away that I would never be Stella's one and only fan. I guess that's sort of what I liked about her: the transerotic honesty that she would never swim with only one man. Stella was the essence of Hollywood where science enhances, and sometimes, reveals, true nature. She was designed for play. Her body was the cove of pleasure for many men.

A crash from the pool house caught my attention. Stella's eyes did not open. Instead, she called out a man's name.

"Jim?"

A young man appeared at the door of the pool house. He was wearing the green teeshirt of a pool cleaning company in Beverly Hills.

"Jim," Stella called, "are you all right?"

The Pool Man turned to the naked woman floating in the bright pool. He squinted in his own dazzle. His hand rubbed his crotch. Pulled at his pants.

This was going to be better than a screentest!

This was in a sense a true test of Stella's sexual athletic ability, of that certain something that clicks physically on the set before it can ever click cinematographically in the camera.

Jim was the perfect leading man. He could have been an X-rated star himself. Stella opened her eyes and stared at him. Her hand moved to her sweet little clit. She smiled up at him cupping himself.

"Rub it for me," she said. "Rub it good and solid and hard for me. Rub it for me. Look at me and rub it for me."

Stella had a good sense for a scene. A feel for it. She might even, I thought, turn into a major director of underground sex films.

"Strip off your shirt," she called. Her voice was smooth and luscious. "Let me see your chest and shoulders. Let me see those strong swimmer's shoulders of yours. Let me see those muscular arms that stroke me, that breast-stroke me so good. Let me see those hard-working hands stroking your swimmer's belly. Let me watch those big hands rub your dick." Her voice trailed off and under the taped sounds of the wild dolphins.

Jim followed Stella's every direction. He seemed awestruck by her shimmering body floating so casually and relaxed in the big pool. He stepped out of his worn torn sneakers.

Stella smiled in the water. Grinned. Flashed her wide smile: red lips and perfect white teeth. Anticipating the long lean fuckdive of this sturdy Pool Man into the water, she rolled from her back to her belly and dived deep down into the pool. Her evenly tanned body arched up. Her perfect buttocks rose poised above the surface. Between her thighs, I could see the triangular patch of her cooze. Smooth skin. Clipped pubes. She dived deep. Her perfectly arched feet pointed her exquisite toes straight up at the sun and sky. Then trailed down into the bubbling water.

The light was so perfect I could see Stella swimming like a fish with long lingering strokes below the surface. Limber arms. Perfect grace. The long lean body of a sea goddess. She had it all. She had it both ways: sea goddess and sea urchin. The perfect Divine Tramp. Just like Marilyn had it on dry land!

Stella was a sport of nature. Something new, different, and hot!

I hoped that her Pool Man had some idea of the kind of Class Act he was about to fuck with.

Stella broke the surface of the water. She seemed, for all her time beneath the surface, to be breathing without any exertion. "Drop your trousers," she called to Jim. "Let me see what I want to see. Let me see what I do to you."

At the side of the pool, Jim unbuckled his pants. His hands fumbled with his belt and zipper. Behind him, a naked statue of Poseidon, God of the Sea, stood, holding his trident, poised under a coat of whitewash. Jim stepped out of his khakis. His tool arched up at an angle tight along his belly.

"You're beautiful," Stella called.

"You're beautiful," he said.

"Fuck me," she whispered.

He walked to the edge of the pool. His toes locked down around the marble lip. His strong legs bent slightly and propelled him straight up into the warm California air. Looking directly at Stella, the Pool Man, hardon roaring against his gut, dived neatly into the water.

Stella dropped her legs low in the water. Her arms and tits and hair floated around her shoulders.

Jim cut like a knife between her legs spinning her

around, holding her strong thighs in his arms, sucking his mouth up against her underwater pussy, tonguing her clit, licking her belly, rimming her butt, rising to her tits, diving to her cunt. Swimming in a frenzy of sexual heat. Turning her. Twisting her. Pulling her down under the water. Pulling Stella's laughing face down down to his dick. Pushing her mouth down on the heavy bait of his hook. Fucking her face in slow-motion deep water thrusts. Breaking the water singularly and together. Clawing wildly. Romping. Two sea animals conjoining in splashy copulation. Making sounds in the water much like the dolphins.

They almost stopped. Floated for a moment. Adrift on the tide of their lust. Their genuine lust. I had watched Stella boil up the lust in the Pool Man. I had watched her boil up the lust in herself. She was no fake who would call for a stand-in. She was the genuine fuckable article.

Jim's mouth went down on her tits. Stella's hands guided the dorsal fin of his erect tool straight toward the sea-cave of her cunt. She teased her clit with his cock head as she teased his cock head with her clit. Rubbing the two together. Then, perfectly positioned, cock-to-cunt, Stella pulled Jim's face up from her bobbing breasts and kissed him hard on the mouth. She opened her lips and felt his tongue pass deep down her throat. She pushed back on his tongue and drove her own tongue deep into his mouth. Together, guided by her hands, they rammed their hips toward one another.

The water exploded like a depth charge between their legs and up their torsos.

Stella's head reared back. She was a seahorse raised

from the water on a trident spear. She cried the cum-cries of the wild dolphins. He roared into her. She clawed into him. They sank beneath the splashing waves. Rose and broke the surface. Sank in one another's arms to the bottom of the pool. For a long time, or for what seemed a long time, they made no sound. Only the recorded cry of the dolphins whinnied in the clear California sunshine. Only thin strands of bubbles rose up slowly from the pair locked in the exhaustion of their love-making on the blue pool bottom.

I figured I'd better leave the way I arrived. No need to embarrass Stella's Pool Stud. No need for her to know what I'd witnessed. So I went back through the bushes, damning myself for not having brought my camera. I drove back to my office and called her on the phone. I said I was sorry I couldn't make it. She said she was sorry too, because she had been exercising and was in top shape to see me. I liked that. Top Shape. Yeah, I said into the phone, for sure.

Months later, when a producer, who had read the press releases I wrote weekly for Stella Maris, needed a scriptwriter for his X-rated version of the old MGM swimming movie *Dangerous When Wet*, Stella suggested me. I wrote the script, or rather ground it out, in three days. The point is that, if you remember the opening sequence from that film, I based it on Stella's afternoon delight with the Pool Man—except, for the erotic sake of the picture, I surrounded Stella with a whole school of mermaids. Lots of wet tits and ass squirming and swimming underwater in glorious Technicolor Cinemascope with dolphins calling and the sounds of bubbles gurgling up their thighs and tits on the Dolby soundtrack.

All six pictures Stella made back-to-back that first year were glossy big production numbers. Stella, from the start, was a high-button act. I saw to that. She begged me to be her manager. I agreed. I had a feel for what the public wanted.

Just like John Derek later directed Bo Derek to rise from the sea in commercial films, I scripted Stella's taste for wet in the world of independent erotic film.

We made money hand over fist. Stella was invited to appear in her mermaid tail on TV's "Tonight Show Tonight." The producer delivered her to the set on a golf cart. She flipped her fins. She wore her long hair down and full over her naked breasts. She was so perfectly modest, and the host, Jay Carson was so genuinely funny about the whole gimmick, that the TV censors missed that Stella wasn't wearing a body stocking.

"This is a major star," Jay Carson said. "She has the kind of chest that puts new meaning into the phrase 'Boob Tube.'" The audience roared. "She's sort of an X-rated *Jaws*. Just when you thought it was safe to go back in the water...no wonder Charlie the Tuna uses the breast-stroke!"

Stella was a hit.

I scripted her next picture to open with an X-rated version of that scene in *From Here to Eternity*, where Burt Lancaster and Deborah Kerr make love on the beach with the waves crashing in on top of them. Stella had written in an entry in her diary that the first time she had cum without touching herself was watching that famous wet scene on late-night TV while her parents were out. She had been entranced with the idea of making love on that margin of sand between real earth and real ocean. She had not been able to control herself when the man and woman were doused with the crashing wet spray and the rolling force of white surf.

Her movies were grossing big at the X-rated box offices. Her name was up in lights. College film societies began to book her films in as underground/underwater cult and camp features. Adult bookstores noted a brisk upsurge in the sale of her movies on 8mm and Super-8 film. The money was rolling in. She was famous the way she wanted to be famous.

I was balling with her every night. I wanted it. She wanted it. She needed it.

One night, laid back on her big heart-shaped waterbed, she said, "I want to do something bigger, better, outrageous. I want to top everything I've done. Everything you've done. I want us to be so fantastic and far out that the world will have a hardon forever. They'll never forget us. I want us to make a movie that will shock the public. Entertain them. Get them off. I want it erotic, beautiful, and very, very, very different. I want to make one last film, one last truly great X-rated spectacle. Then I will retire forever from films. Just one great last big splash. Will you write it for me?"

I got up from the waterbed. Her firm, warm body had left traces of its secret moist smells on my mouth and hands and dick. I could smell her hot musk dampness on my body. I walked over to the cold salt water aquarium tank that gurgled under hidden fluorescent lights against the far wall.

"Will you think up something special for me? Please. For this one great last movie."

I drew a blank. She was right. We had to make one

last shot at a picture that would play the theaters longer than *Deep Throat*. There's only so much anyone can
do in a career before they start repeating themselves.
Stella and I never wanted to do the same thing twice.
Never.

"Something different. New. Outrageous. Something
shocking. Something so mixed with terror and beauty
that audiences won't be able to take their eyes off the
screen." Stella rose like a goddess off the waterbed. She
walked to me by the aquarium. Her long graceful fingers
touched my cheek, my chest, my belly, my dick, my balls.
"I love you," she said. "I think I love you." She raised her
hand. Her fingernails were manicured and painted a
deep aquamarine. "I want to be better than James Bond
in his movies. I want to do it everywhere and anyway I
can underwater." She raised her graceful arm and slowly dipped her tanned white hand into the cold saltwater
aquarium. Her nail polish glowed iridescent among the
sealife in the fluorescent tank.

"It doesn't matter," I said.

"What?" She moved her hand toward a sea anemone. She fingered its spongy filaments.

"Love," I said. "It doesn't matter in an X-rated
world."

Stella's mouth formed a small bee-sting pout.
Thoughtfully, she fingered into the nickel-sized opening
of the anemone. "I suppose," she said, "it doesn't." She
circled her finger around the soft tentacles of the anemone. She poked down into its dark hole, stroking the simple sea creature, causing it to open wider, fingering it to
full open bloom, masturbating its soft wet tissues until its
dark pink inside rolled its lips back in a gaping shudder of

primitive orgasm. She slipped almost all of her small delicate hand into the briny thing's thrusting hole. Its tentacles rose and fell with the tidal pump of the water, licking around her wrist. "You're right," she said. She smiled into the tank, feeling the sea creature's cool mucous membranes orgasming around her warm hand. "This is all that matters."

"Come on back to bed," I said. "Let's fuck."

Stella was a creature of wild animal passion. She could never get enough.

"I want it all," she screamed while she was coming. "I want it all."

Sometime during our restless sleep that night the idea for Stella's ultimate screenplay came to me. Nothing blinding. Nothing flashy. Just an image of a sea anemone being stroked open to full acceptance of a gentle hand that probed its tight, dark depths. In the morning, when Stella awoke, with all the innocence of a small girl made pure and rested by sleep, she saw me sitting outside the sliding glass bedroom doors by the side of the shimmering blue pool.

"So this is how screenwriters do it," she said. She kissed my shoulder and padded barefoot across the blue-green tile to the pool edge where she stretched the full length of her lithe blonde body. Her butt was spectacular in the clear morning sun. My tongue wanted to rim her ass forever. "First dip!" she called, and dived into the water like some angel plunging from the heights. Her body, rippling through the water, made my tool stand at full attention. She surfaced at the end of the pool, spewed water out from between her perfect white teeth like the strong athlete she was, and said, "I may not love you, but

I sure love your dick."

"And my dick loves you," I said. "Stop bothering me. I'm writing a fast treatment for the erotic movie of the century."

"Far out!" she yelped and dived under the surface like a playful porpoise.

Three weeks later, with backers all in line, and the best technical film crew that Hollywood could muster, we were ready to roll the cameras. The arrangement for the special underwater location had been surprisingly easy. It was time for Scene One/Take One on the first day of filming *Slippery When Wet*. The script was dynamite. Audiences would remember Stella Maris forever.

The producer had a lech for Stella. She could do no wrong. And he was right. Somehow, she was that rare creature—the full-grown woman who was not a Tinseltown bitch on wheels. And where Stella was concerned, the producer wrote *carte blanche*. Even I, in his eyes, could do no wrong. He gave us a blank check to shoot what we liked.

"You know what Stella can handle. And I figure you know," the producer said, "what audiences will pay their money to see. So do it. I don't care if you want to hire a hundred pretty girls and rent ninety-nine beautiful costumes. If Stella really intends to retire after this picture, then we've got to wrap up a classic showpiece no man alive will ever forget!" He groped himself and laughed. "Tits and ass, man. Under glass. Tits and ass. Underwater. What a combination! What a gimmick!"

"As long as there's a market for skin at the box office, Stella wants to give them the best action there is. She knows it's porn. She calls it erotic art. So she wants to lay it out with style. Stella," I said, "is a class act."

And she was. She showed up every day, fit as a trooper, going through the long and difficult takes of the shooting schedule. Learning her lines. Keeping tempers cool on the set. Fucking only with four or five of the college swimmers and water-polo jocks hired as brawny extras in the underwater fantasy sequences. The tricks that girl showed some of those college boys, I'll tell you, really blew their socks off.

Stella had great respect for the lights and the camera. She had even greater respect for the action. On camera and off.

"Fucking keeps my spirits up," she said. "Every actress rehearses for her role. And my role calls for serious fucking. A girl needs all the help she can get. Right?"

Almost up to the day of shooting the last big underwater scene, the casting director had not found the right type of stud to play opposite Stella. Casting a male in a fuckfilm causes some complications. Especially when the film takes place underwater. The guy has to be almost an Olympic swimmer as well as a good-looking stud who can keep a hardon in front of the cameras. On top of that, I figured I had Stella's feelings to consider. Sure. She's a pro, I thought. Actresses don't always like their leading men. But in Hollywood films, that doesn't matter. They're only kissing mouth-to-mouth. The tricks Stella performed with her leading men were much more intimate. A honey like Stella deserved the best meat on the studio lot.

Slippery When Wet was into its second week of shooting Stella's underwater nude swimming with a bevy of about twenty other topless mermaids swinging their fishy tails at the camera. The Assistant Director said he was getting worried. "We're three days behind shooting schedule," he said. "We can't keep working around the fact that there's no actor cast for the final fuck sequence."

"We're trying," I said. "We haven't hit on the right combination."

"What combination?" He took a long drag on his Maduro cigar. "This is a fuck movie. Not *Gone With The Wind*. We need an All-American guy. We're not looking for Scarlett O'Hara."

Right on cue, Stella came through. "Look what I found," she said. Her hair was slightly disheveled. Her eyes looked bright, eager, and hot to fuck. "This hunk of man," she said, "is my new Aqua-Stud." She pulled the guy, who was sort of standing head and shoulders behind her, around to her side.

"Who is he?" the producer asked.

"He's been working with the crew. He's majoring in film at USC. He's been on the set since shooting started. You could say I've been auditioning him. He's the Best Boy. Actually, I think he's the best man. I want him..."

"You've had him," the producer said.

"...in this picture. In the last sequence. He's perfect for the Aqua-Fuck scene."

The guy stood there smiling like a gambler with a royal flush. Stella took control of the whole audition. She unbuttoned his shirt and pulled it off his chest and shoulders. He was built. Powerful. Good jock body. She ran her soft hand across the light hair on his chest. Her other hand rumpled the hair on his head. She was a woman who knew the geography of a man's body. She flipped open the top button of his Levi's and slipped her hand down into his crotch. Her tongue circled her lips in deliberate concentration. The guy stood still while she manipulated him. She loosened his jeans and dropped them from around his muscular waist. His tool sprang up. She cupped his balls in her hand.

He was a definite rival for John Holmes.

"Do you want to call the *Guinness Book of World Records?*" Stella asked the producer, "or should I?"

She helped the guy step out of his jeans. He stood naked under the producer's examination. His piece rose straight up against his belly. Stella leaned into him. She pressed her pussy against his thigh. His dick stuck up higher than his navel. She laid her blonde head against his swimmer's powerful chest. He could have been a quarterback at any Super Bowl. "He's perfect," she said. "And he's no Hollywood fag. He's straight. God almighty! Is he ever straight. He's a nonstop straight fucking genuine exhibitionist!"

The big guy smiled.

"He does have a certain early Clint Eastwood quality," the producer said. "I suppose, with the references he has from your auditioning him, that he'll do."

"He'll more than do," Stella said.

And more than do he did. And so did Stella. The climax of *Slippery When Wet* started out with twenty big-boobed Aqua-Nymphettes gliding in synchronized strokes past the big underwater Cinemascope camera. As the girls churn through their routine, Stella swims into the picture. She's pursued by the Aqua-Stud. She outraces him for awhile, teasing him, darting back around his legs, skimming past his dick. He thinks he is in pursuit of her. Really she is about to capture him. On a signal from Stella, the Aqua-Nymphettes close in and trap the Aqua-Stud in a swirl of nets. Bubbles rise up around his body as the mermaids wind him and bind him in their nets and poke at his body with their spears. Stella swims overhead as he struggles. The nets cinch him tighter. The Aqua-Nymphettes tow his struggling body toward a metal shark-cage submerged in the depths of the waters. He is helpless against them. He is locked in the iron cage, naked, with only a twist of net wrapped around his body. Nearby, small but playful sand sharks cruise the waters in their hungry search for sex and food. Stella swims among them, unharmed, like the ruling goddess of the underwater world.

This, remember, is Hollywood where anything is possible.

When the Second Assistant Director called, "Quiet on the set," Stella stood on the rim of the massive filming tank. She was posed naked with only a large sea flower in her blonde hair. The Still Photographer silently clicked off several rolls of color film for publicity release. The only mags interested in stills from Stella's first movie had been sleaze-rags. Now, one year and six hit films later, I figured Stella was on her way to the cover of *Time*. She had the mix of high pizazz and innocence that turned boys into men and men into animals. When the Second Assistant Director shouted, "Roll 'em," Stella looked down into the water. Her Aqua-Stud was caged down among the sand sharks. She smiled. The Love Goddess of X-Rated Underwater Extravaganzas smiled, and dived like a knife in the water, trailing streams of bubbles in a shimmering halo around her nude body.

She swam gracefully through the sharks, stroking their lazy backs, rolling and turning, graceful long arms pulling her through the depths, her long blonde hair streaming behind her head. She cruised slowly behind the iron bars of the fuck-cage. The man trapped inside swam in long circles. He watched her push her pussy up to the bars. He swam toward her. He ate her out. Tongued her. Licked her. A sand shark hovered curiously around her ankles. Another shark approached and the two sharks sped away nipping and nibbling at one another. Stella pushed her cooze into his face. She placed her knees through the bars. Her tits pressed against the metal and bobbed around over his head while he ate her out. His tool rose big, leaking sea-pearls of pre-cum. The camera man looked through his lens and saw the dick magnified through the water. "Fuckin' whale meat," he said.

Stella had a way of making all her sex mates feel huge with her. She managed to maintain a firm tightness that made men grow to enormous size. She brought out a lust in males that made them potent and long lasting fuckmachines. What she did on camera with her leading men, she did on screen to the guys watching her in the theater rows. When Stella's movies played the adult theaters, the aisles streamed with jism. She was a two-or-three-cum hit with audiences who appreciated getting their money's worth, and then some, for the price of admission.

Stella opened the door of the steel cage and swam inside, circling around the Aqua-Stud's body. She hovered over his dick and chest. She bobbed suggestively. Her clipped blonde twat touched down hot on the head of his meat. She worked her labial lips like gills over his dick. Her lip control was famous at the box office. She could work over a dick with those lips that were slicker than a hand job. The camera tracked in for a close-up. The screen bloomed with the wild pink flesh of her blonde juicy cunt. Her clit roared up crazy and red. Stray bubbles rushed from her furry pussy shaved back just enough to reveal the full lip action of her labia reaming off the head of his gigantic tool.

Around her the water was deep blue-green. Underwater spotlights threw a rosy flesh glow over her flawless skin. She dropped her incredible tits down toward his face. Her butt and legs floated smooth and lithe in the water. He pulled her to him. And the fucking started. Stella liked hard balling in real life. She liked it even wilder on film. She was rhythmic. Perfect. Total in her passion with this built-and-hung exhibitionist. She liked to be fucked hard and deep. She liked the feel of monster cock nibbling up against her clit while it plowed her into deep ecstasy. She guided him where she wanted him. She took charge of their fuck. He was her fuck-captive in the script. He had no way on the set to act but to follow her wild lead and ad-lib moves as she tormented and tested the prowess of his hardon exhibition. He knew that to fuck with Stella Maris was to build a reputation as a stud second to none. He had heard that this was her greatest and last picture. He knew that he had been cast to fuck her crazy at her cinematic peak. He knew that he wanted this woman. Camera or not. He knew that his lust for her would shine on screen and millions of men would pant for her the way he hungered for her. He knew that women would identify with her and dream about him fucking them unconscious.

He drove his dick into her with a vengeance. Stella made wild cooing sounds in the water. Sharks darted.

Excited. The pump of their fucking rocked the shells and seaweed decorating the natural-looking underwater set. He held her by the shoulders and raised her legs, floating her back in the water. She was weightless. He put his hands on her hips and pulled her sleek body down on his dick. Again and again, he lifted her off and pulled her down hard on his dick. Ramming her. Jamming her. Fucking her. With mighty thrusts. Her hair floated in wild streams around her face. Her mouth opened and closed. Her eyes rolled back and closed. And he maintained like some incredible deep sea diver. Pumping her. Humping her. Pulling her down on his dick. Eating her tits. Chawing on her. Making raw primitive bubbles burst out of her fucked-raw cunt, out of her mouth.

"Cheezuz. Gawd," the producer whispered.

"She loves it," I said.

"You should know." He turned to me. "We'll be lucky if we even get a triple-X rating multiplied by triple-X."

Stella wrapped her arms around the young Aqua-Stud's head. She squeezed his face into her double-barreled breasts. She mashed her cunt down on his dick. Her tongue sought his mouth, pushed through his lips and teeth. He felt her slick warm tongue slip serpentinely down his throat. She fucked him back. Stroke for stroke. She clenched her cunt down tight on him. Holding him hardon captive inside her cooze. She rubbed her clit on the upper root of his dick. Her belly was tight against his. He could feel the full trimness of her seductive body.

On cue, Stella arched her butt. She pulled herself up and almost off his enormous dick. The special effects crew hit their electronic units. Once. Twice. Three times. She lifted off and then slam dunked her cunt down on his dick. Ramming him deep into her. Again and again. Her soft lips set firm and passionate. Fucking her man crazy. Honestly wanting to stroke his cum from deep inside his balls and dick. The special effects shot off exactly as his load was breaking loose somewhere behind his eyes in his head. Colored smoke bombs spewed up in the water surrounding the cage. The sand sharks swam wildly around the cage bars. His load sped down his spine and past the small of his back. Underwater flares shot off like sparklers. His nuts knotted up and shot into his dick. He pumped deep into her. She pushed hard onto him. Porpoises swam past. Aqua-Nymphettes dived and rose through the sharks. Her lips tightened down on him. She sucked his juices, wet and white, deep into her dark crevice. Her head reared back in wild abandon. Her cunt shot shock waves erupting out her every nerve ending and synapse.

The producer was ecstatic. "Three cameras shooting at one time. Count 'em. Three cameras. Shit. This is going to be the fuck-footage of the century!"

Stella pulled back. She looked at her Aqua-Stud. Face to face. He kissed her tits and tongued down her throat. His hands caught in a wild tangle of her hair. Then he lifted her bodily. Up and off his cock. She rose floating in the water. Full of his cum. Smiling with the exhaustion of her multiple thrashing orgasms. She floated in his arms.

An underwater cameraman swam in close for a two-shot of Aqua-Stud holding Stella's body. He came in close to her twat and belly. Stella knew the cue. She flexed her hips and butt. She concentrated on her cunt. She forced his cum back down toward her lips. Slowly, in full range

of the camera, she ejected the white clots of his hot jism.
The white stuff came up out of her immaculate cunt like
angels' food. Stella floated back in absolute peace. One
after the other, three Aqua-Nymphettes swam over the
two resting bodies. They nipped at the white cum floating in the blue green water. Their tongues licked and
nipped at the strings of white jism. They fed on the aqua-
seed passed between the Stud and the Nymph.

In the last and final shot of *Slippery When Wet*, the
camera closed in on Stella's cunt. There, in its full glory,
in the tight grip of her strong labial lips, lay a flawless
and perfect pearl. The underwater light made it shim-
mer with iridescence. The smooth look of it tempted every man who saw the film to dive down for this cunt pearl
of great price.

The rest, as they say, is history.

Stella doesn't make movies any more. She's dab-
bling in producing some films. Who knows? Hollywood
stars don't make as many movies as they used to. But
every once in a while they come back to the screen with
a big hit. I figure maybe that's what Stella might do. In
the meantime, *Slippery When Wet* continues to break box
office records around the world. Stella made her fantasy
come true. Audiences never felt she was dirty. Something
special about her made them indulgent and forgiving
about her X-rated rise to the super stardom of being an
international celebrity and personality. Women thought
she was daring. Men loved her and lusted after her. And
I just keep on keeping on playing around with all the wet
dreams of my very own Aqua-Nymph.

My dad said, "Your way in the world
will be easier if you remember
most people prefer masculine men,
straight or gay,
masculine in the best sense,
not macho in the worst."

TALES FROM
THE BEAR CULT:
BUZZ SPAULDING'S
TRAINING ACADEMY

MASSIVE! My dad was built big like a cocky power
lifter. He was a local construction trucker. Hard-
bodied bear, bearded, athletic burly Look, handsome as
all outdoors, and hung a full third-of-a-yard. Inside the
thick neck of his blue collar, he was a laidback free spirit. As a kid, I imagined he worked as a pro wrestler, not
the comic-book ugly villains, but one of the broad-shoul-
dered, thick-armed heroes, armored by his big, but tight,
hairy belly, standing on legs like twin oaks.

I grew up loving his Power Look.

Some guys whose taste is no wider than *Gentleman's Quarterly* have a hard time understanding that not
every man who loves men likes them garbed and groomed

to the 9's and 10's, all gussied up with underarm deodorant, mousse, shaved chests, and 32-inch inseams. Me? I like men big. I want to be one. I intend to get as big as I can. Not just so I can play some ball in college, but so I can make my dick as big as it can be pumped and stretched.

Mention "Bears" to some men and they go crazy: hairy, powerfully built men, usually bearded, maybe a little attractively balding, thick furry forearms and hands, the kind of horsehung men who, if they were centaurs, would be Clydesdales. My dad was the picture of bear-solid manhood, right down to his dick. Built as big as he was, he was gifted with a massive cock that jutted out below his belly and hung stallion thick down between his thunder thighs.

He was a man's man okay. He worked out at the sweaty gym in the unventilated basement of the local Y and I used to go with him, not knowing why, not knowing what homosexuality was, unable even as a kid to imagine in my innocence what two men could do. Shoot! I only knew I got this fainting, dying feeling watching all those big-bodied bearmen strutting around the locker room, stark, buck, naked. Not comprehending what I really wanted, I translated my feelings into an aching prayer, Oh please, dear God, I want to be like him, him, no—him, no—all of them when I grow up. My genes, however, came out 60-40, my mom's side of the family beating out my dad, no matter that he shot me out his big stud cock.

"You're built fine," he consoled me, "like a swimmer."

I blanched. Swimming wasn't my sport. I dreamed of tough football in college, sleek bodybuilding after graduation, and bearded powerlifting when I came into full maturity. But there we were naked, dad and I, alone at the house, after jogging. It was my last summer before starting college. I'd graduated high school the night before. All of a sudden, he was telling me the facts of life, a bit late, but dads always put it off until they absolutely feel they have to actually talk about it. I took advantage of the situation. "But mine's not big enough," I said, fishing for a complement and a compliment.

He smiled and took my 8-inch soft-on in his hand. Nothing feels better than your dad's big paw holding your cock, then guiding your rod right next to his, holding them side by side, inch for inch. He took my hand and wrapped his fingers into mine around our cocks. This wasn't sex. It was sex education of the best kind. It was reassurance. My dick was big enough to cause my asshole buddies to kid me in the shower, but it wasn't anywhere near my dad's size 12. "How'd you get so big?" I asked.

"There's ways."

"Tell me. Tell me how I can get big. I take after mom's side."

"Maybe a little more than my side, but you're my son. If you want to get big, I can make you get big."

"Can I pack on some shoulders and some big pecs like yours?

"You can have anything you want. You want big forearms and massive biceps? Shoot! You can add inches on anywhere you have a mind to."

"My mind is in my dick."

"Like father, like son," he said. "I know a man. He's a kind of coach."

"What kind of coach?"

"A Power Coach. He can work you over thoroughly. He can change your body image completely. A dick coach. A coach who stretches eager penises, who Vaselines tender cock and slips it into a vacuum pump that sucks the dick longer and wider than you ever thought possible. I've worked with him. I go to him once a month. Have for years. Just to keep the pump he puts into my dick. Check out these massive veins." He put my fingers on his cock. "I put on 3 inches in length my first year with him."

"What'd mom think?"

"She sings soprano while she does the dishes."

My dick was hardening down the length of my father's cock.

"I didn't know you were like that," he said. He meant my hardon. He meant my liking us dick-to-dick. He meant, suddenly discovering it, my liking men like that.

"So what." I said. I was ready for a fight. He raised me to be a wise ass.

"So nothing. It's your life. It's cool. I'm just a dumb dad. I never guessed. You're so much like me every way else. It's cool. Really. I should have noticed."

"Relax," I said. "I just noticed it myself a couple months ago."

"Is it good for you? I often wonder what it would be like, but I'm true to your mom." He blushed. "Kind of corny these days, huh? Neither man nor gal nor sleet of night can tear me away from that woman."

My dad was the one who was cool. Guys, even more than women, were always propositioning him, and if the truth be known, he liked it, taking it as the complement and compliment a proposition truly is, especially him being so provocative, parading around the locker room at the Y like a big hairy bear on patrol, padding naked into the steam room, sitting, knees wide apart, sweat pouring down his hairy pecs and big hard belly and dripping off his 12-inch cock hanging thick and veined over the lip of white-grouted tile.

He wrote down the name of the Coach Buzz Spaulding, and handed it to me. "You're what? Six foot, 170? You want to get up to 195 to, say, 215? You want inches on your arms and chest? You want a nice tight gut at your age that can fill out when you're mine? You want a pro cocksman to take your dick and lengthen it and widen it, you call that number. You tell him you're my son. I'll handle everything."

Our dick's were still entwined in our hands. Mine was hard.

"Straight or gay," my dad said, "you're still a man. One's not better than the other, but the only thing I'll tell you is your way in the world will be easier if you remember most people prefer masculine men, straight or gay, masculine in the best sense, not macho in the worst." He laughed and let go of my hand and my cock. "Fuck! I sound like a 38-year-old fart talking through Ann Landers' dentures."

"What am I going to do with this?" I pointed at my cock.

"Terminal hardon?" he said. "Lie back. Here comes the Terminator."

My God! No kid thinks his dad is this liberal. Naked he stood over me, my dad the Bear, facing me, then he squatted down over my hips and spread his hairy powerpacker thighs across my abdominals.

"Don't touch me," he said. "The feelings inside you aren't inside me. But I understand. You're my boy. Just look at me. Study me. Memorize what you see. Internalize it. Straight or gay, I want my son to grow up as much like his dad as possible."

"Okay," I said, never letting up. "But can I jerk off?"

He smiled down at me, and like a boyhood dream come true, he raised up to one knee as I slid my hand past the long firehose of his cock, underneath his studballs, past the furry pucker of his asshole, and took my cock in my hand, stroking it, watching him rub his big palms across the paired pecs of his big upholstered chest, sliding down his hairy belly, palming the hair on his forearms, raising his arms into a double biceps shot, the sweat beading up in the thick furze of his armpits, then rubbing his hands through his short thick beard, defining his strong jawline.

He was teaching me how to image, man-to-man, about being a man, about how a man enjoys his own body, no matter his sexual preference. He was telling me, when a man, like a young college-bound athlete dedicates himself to getting big, then nothing else exists but big, getting big, eating big, working out big, buying bigger and bigger clothes, walking big through the mall, taking over a room with bigness, big shoulders, massive chest, huge arms, powerful thighs, dynamic calves, big jock bubblebutt, but most of all, the center of it all, the handle of the universe, the big hunk of tube steak swinging long and fat and ready for erection when a gangly kid in his teens fills out, hanging out in the gyms and the dorms, and becomes a Big Man on Campus in his twenties.

He rubbed his hands on his pecs, then ran one down to his big soft penis, and picked it up, because the head of his cock had been dragging on my belly. Seeing that big dick cradled in his hairy fingers, I came, careful not to splash my load on the furry cheeks of his butt.

He squeezed my jaw in his big hand. His biceps bulged. His hairy pecs mounded as he squeezed me. "That's my boy," he said. "I am what I am. You are what you are." He released the pressure. "Go get big," he said. "And don't trim that moustache. Grow it big."

A week later I checked into Buzz Spaulding's Training Camp. Buzz had played pro football for six years as a linebacker before a cash offer he couldn't refuse lured him to the Professional Wrestling Federation. The rich backer who hired him on wasn't interested so much in what Buzz could do in the ring as in what he could do for the "pro-gladiators" in the Federation.

Size was the name of the game. Wrestlers. Footballers. Recruit 'em younger. Train 'em harder. Grow 'em bigger. Unleash 'em into pro sports. Buzz got an underground reputation. He was turning boys into men and men into giants with one interesting side effect none of his proteges could stop bragging about. Almost any strength-camp coach could, in a year, turn a 5-7, 170-pound kid into a 220-pound fireplug with 22-inch arms, or a 6-2, 200 man into a 275-pound no-neck behemoth who'd make Hulk Hogan and Arnold take notice.

What no one did, the way Buzz Spaulding did, was make cocks grow big, bigger, massive!

Buzz Spaulding had invented the better mouse trap and the world was beating off a path to his door. If Buzz and my dad hadn't gone way back, I'd never have gotten into the Training Camp of my dreams.

My first night in the dorm, I was too green, too excited, too hardon for action to sleep, so I did what any normal 18-year-old horny kid would do. I left my room to prowl the premises, cruising the other rooms with open doors, seeing guys of all ages, kids my age to big dudes in their thirties, all of them obviously Power Jocks, and from the looks I got at some of the cocks, flopped out soft, or hard, in sleep, Coach Buzz Spaulding's famous Side Effect was working. If my dad told me so, it was so. My dick hardened wanting to meet Buzz Spaulding first chance. I was gonna be one big motherfucker.

Downstairs, in the gym, the "Night Crew," guys who liked the concentration of the hours after midnight, were working out, some nude, some in jockstraps, some in football grey cotton teeshirts cut off right below the pecs, all in sweaty leather weight belts and heavy black leather combat boots to grip the rubber mats better for steadier lifts. They were banging the weights, grinding out heavy sets, pulling at their cocks that were light years beyond any cocks I'd ever seen in high school.

The average hang was 9 inches to maybe 14 inches. Soft. I later found out the way Buzz measured cock: twice. Once soft. Once hard. Starting from the top of the base at the belly to the tip of the piss slit for the length, and then the circumference halfway up the shaft. So a cock wasn't just 10 inches long. It was, somewhat like a 2x4 piece of lumber or a 4x4 truck, judged by length and circumference. A 10-inch cock with a 9-inch circumference was a 10x9, or 90 square inches of dick. Strut! Strut! Strut! Do the Pete Rose Grope! No wonder, jocks in every sport, once they've been to Camp, strut like they're

God's gift to man.

I ducked into the toilet opposite the weight room, and even though the stalls had no doors, I dropped my jock around my ankles, and plopped my butt on the black horseshoe. Hearing the serious weights crashing, listening to the *goddamshitfuckpiss* and the kidding around, my dick kind of jumped up into my hand crying for a lube job. "Hey, little fella," I said, "you're 8x6 tonight and I'm 170. In a month of training, who knows how big we'll be. Me, maybe 190. You 10x8!"

My butt stung where an assistant coach had shot me with my first dose of a new designer steroid with no side effects. "Even if there was a sidekicker, like there was in the old days," my dad had counseled me, "you have to make up your mind whether you want quality of life or quantity of life." He touched my shoulder. "Don't worry. Buzz has doctors monitoring everything from your liver to your bodyfat to your sperm count. Just do what he says. Anything he says."

Imaging myself growing as big and hung and muscular as the Night Crew, I was beating my cock right to the cusp of cuming, when, O sweet jumpin Jack Flash, these pair of knees, followed by massive tanned thighs covered with curly blond hair slid under the partition, presenting in the valley between their bulk a pair of hefty blond balls and a hardon the size wet dreams are made on. Fucking 13 inches. A 13x10, I figured. My butthole puckered in fear. No way could my ass jam that log. If I chowed down on it, I figured I'd choke to death, and all my mourners would die of jealousy.

The hard blond cock throbbed and bobbed, patient, waiting, seeming to grow another inch. It wasn't going away. The stud attached to it had made a commit he wasn't backing away from when he shoved his power thighs under the partition. He was big and I didn't want any trouble.

All I could do was take his rockhard pillar of velvet smoothness into my hands. I cupped my palms around it and drooled down some foamy spit. The big blond dick itself seeped clear lube. What a beauty for a handjob. The guy started pumping his hips up and down. From the side, I could see his perfect bubble butt. He looked to weigh in at a buffed 225. I figured if he was this good-looking from the waist down, he must be a knockout north of the border.

"Put both hands on it," he said. His deep voice came from his big balls. "I want you to pull me off, and when I start cuming I want your mouth as far down on it as you can suck."

I fell to my knees on the cool toilet floor. Buzz Spaulding's Bulk Dick formula not only enlarged even the most average cock to remarkable size; it also kept the cocks buzzed, which explained his nickname. No one ever heard of a Buzz Spaulding dick ever having trouble, the way some monster dicks have, of staying hard. I wrapped both my hands around the mystery cock with plenty left over for my lips and mouth and throat. I went to town. Hungry for big dick. Wanting the bulk load from the bulked dick of the buffed stud offering me what I dreamed of. The more of his seed I swallowed, the faster I'd get bigger. I turned maniac, dipping, bowing, blowing, sucking, rimming the corona, tubing the fat head and shaft deeper than I'd ever swallowed anything but food before.

"Hey! Hey! Hey!" he said. "Watch the teeth."

"Sorry." I mumbled with my mouth full.

He pulled his butt back, taking his glorious thighs and splendid erect cock back under the metal toilet partition. I figured I'd lost him.

"Let's try it another way," he said. He stood before me. Framed naked in the doorway. Both hands on his dick. He was a god. A blond, built, Bear God. I lost my mind. He was perfect. He was a man. He had a man's strength and fragility, a man's grace and intensity, a good-looking man's full-bodied muscle.

"Yes," I said. To him I could say nothing but *yes*. One thing I knew for sure. I knew it from my dad. From living with him. I knew for sure that nature very rarely puts it all together: looks, bearing, voice, appeal, smile, intelligence, strength. Rugged face. Massive muscles. Monster cock. Honest manliness is never half-revealed. When it's there, it's all right there in front of you. Especially when the 13x10-inch hardon won't go down. I sat my butt back on the black horseshoe toilet seat. My mouth leveled with his cock.

He took one step toward me. His dick rose like the prow on a Viking ship. His nipples were honeytan and circled by the blond hair on the mounded slabs of his pecs. He didn't have a belly: he had abs so carved their crevasses showed through the blond belly hair that was a darker blond than his golden regulation-clipped moustache. His 130-square-inch dick poled out from a patch of curly blond brillo that was the same blond as his perfect butch-waxed flat top. For openers, I wanted to rub my hard cock through the thick hair on his forearms.

I fisted my dick with one hand. He smiled and

moved closer. He smelled of sweet salt sweat. I reached out to his cock and touched the tip. "Go on," he said. He ran one hand up his torso and wiped out his massive armpit, then fed me his sweaty fingers and palm, making a fist and pushing it like a gentle boxer against my lips, forcing them open, fingering past my teeth, working his big bodybuilder fist into my mouth. I sucked his hand, knowing he was training me. If I could swallow his fist, I could swallow his cock.

He pulled his wet fist out and licked his hand. He stepped toward me, his cock entering my lips, parting my teeth, passing over my tongue. The corona filled my mouth big as a Florida orange. He pumped his shaft hard. The circle of his thumb and forefinger around his cock punched into my lips over my teeth. He was more rugged than rough. Spit ran from my loaded mouth and dripped on my cock my own hand was working. He put both his hands behind my head and started his facefuck ram into my throat. His rod pushed the head deep past my first gag reflex and he rode on in and down slow and easy, pushing in, pulling out, going for the inches. He was well on in 8 inches, with 5 inches to go; that was more than I'd ever taken; but when a handsome man wants to measure off 13 klicks down my throat, I'll be the man my daddy expected.

A couple guys from the Night Crew came in to take a leak. Nobody said a word. At Buzz Spaulding's Training Camp, whatever was, was.

With his cock buried down my throat, he raised his big arms, crossing them below his chest, nippling his pecs with his fingers. The more he twisted at his tits the harder he pushed his prick into me. I wished he'd tattooed inch marks on his cock so I could read below my nose. Four inches left. I couldn't swallow. I could hardly breath. My dick was dangerously near cuming. I looked up at him. His face was in ecstasy.

From his dick pulsing in my throat, I knew he was close to cuming. I whacked my own stroker to keep pace. He leaned forward and drilled another inch down my throat. I felt something tear, but I knew it was no more than the stretching open of another inch of deep virgin throat. He was making me bigger.

Slow, with a suctioning pull, he drew his plunger from my pipe. His big jock body went into muscle lock-down, like a bodybuilder on stage. His dick pulsing, cuming up my throat, into my mouth, already white seed shooting on my tongue, him pulling his dick free, with 13x10 inches shooting sperm hot across my face, burning my eyes, shooting up my nose, filling my open mouth. Even the loads were bigger at the camp. My own hand kept pulling on my dick. I wanted to look at him, to worship him, to image him the way my dad had taught me, so I could grow big as him.

He stood stock still, breathing heavy. His huge horsecock still erect. His balls were massive and crawling one over the other. White cum dripped from his piss slit. I was crazy with lust. I wanted him to piss all over me sitting on the black horseshoe seat.

Instead, he said. "Stop."

"I'm gonna cum."

"I said, *stop*."

It was the hardest order I ever obeyed.

"You don't cum. Not until tomorrow. Tomorrow," he said, "is a special day for you."

"What do you mean?"

"Tomorrow's your day." He flipped his dick, wiped the wet cum on it across my moustache, turned around, pushed his perfect bubblebutt in my face for a fast sweet sniff of his crack and hole, and left.

"Jeez!" I said, sitting on a toilet between a rock and a hardon. "What am I gonna do with this?" My dick stuck up like it would never go down.

One of the Night Crew had been watching all along. "That's the idea," he said. "Discipline. Control. Growth."

"Who the fuck was that?" I asked.

"You know who, and you'll know better tomorrow after your first session."

"Yeah," I guessed, "I know who."

We said his name together. "Buzz Spaulding."

The powerlifter grinned at me. "Hey, kid! Welcome to Bulk City! Now, come and do me."

There's a Summer Place
at Bear Lake...
A one-sentence romance.

THREE BEARS IN A TUB

Listen here, boy, there'll be no hibernatin till after I finish tellin you this bedtime story about Big Daddy when he was himself hardly more than a boy and how he turned into a six-foot-five man and what he done to earn that reputation he got that famous summer on Bear Lake when the canoe overturned late around midnight and Big Daddy on his thirty-fifth birthday saw them two young hairy fishermen floppin like bears in the water next to drownin with their rubber boots suckin them down to the clear rock bottom and them able to stand just barely with their chins on the surface of the moonlit water cuz Bear Lake as you know ain't that deep but deep enough that Griz and Cub was standin so chin deep both their beards was floatin around their heads and all of Big Daddy's two hundred and fifty fucky pounds standin spread-legged on the dock thought even if it was the funniest gutbuster sight he ever saw he better climb on into his rowboat without so much as puttin on a stitch of clothes to cover his hide he was always so proud was so well upholstered that way with a coat of thick fur that

grew out of his toes and wrapped up his foot to his ankle
and grew up his calves like somethin you could curry with
a brush especially near his pair of big thighs that made
his powerful packed legs a sight to see especially if you
caught a lordly eyeful of him come strollin butt naked
out of the two-hole outhouse he had downwind from his
log cabin up on Bear Lake which could happen since Big
Daddy always walked around like a big built hairy man
is God's gift which I suppose is true with no supposin
after all us seein Big Daddy standin lathered up next to
his cabin under that shower with the tub of hot rainwa-
ter he tied up on the roof where the sun could always
shine so he could scrub up his hairy crack he said where
the sun never shined except I know different but that's
another story about harvestin dingleberries if you fud-
gin know what they are and I do appreciate Big Daddy's
hairy butt cheeks and sweet sweaty hairy crack where
there never was one of those little ingrown hairs cuz Big
Daddy always rough-buffed his fur with a big ol towel
which them two handsome boys Griz and Cub could have
used while they was waitin still sinkin in the middle of
Bear Lake next to drownin with the little waves lappin
around their mouths and their beards and long hair floatin in the water cuz of Big Daddy sittin naked in his wood
rowboat in the moonlight lookin down and laughin at the
two heads floatin on the water and them yellin *Keerist,
Big Daddy* cuz everybody always called Big Daddy *Big
Daddy* ever since he done sired Griz when he was sev-
enteen out of that sweet Kathleen Jones over the other
side of Bear Lake and never bothered to marry cuz her
father was one of them shaggy men who takes a side-
wise shine at life and don't care if a young man rolls

his daughter in the hay as long as he gets to roll the fucker himself the way he tried everyone knows to roll over on Big Daddy but Big Daddy rolled over on him and shagged him holdin him by his hair and forcin his mouth open and then his ass all the time shoutin that there was room on Bear Lake for only one Big Daddy and the cum was rollin down Kathleen's legs at the same time it was rollin out the hairy butt and down the hairy legs of her pa and they both was screamin for Big Daddy at first to stop fuckin them and then not to stop fuckin them and that night was a night everyone heard about and no one forgot mostly because nine months later little Griz popped out of Kathleen and some months later out popped Cub makin Big Daddy a real big daddy twice which he said was enough for him so he gave up screwin Kathleen and just kept on screwin her pa who by the way is famous for his moonshine still which he drinks from frequently always namin the praises of Big Daddy who he calls his son-in-law except no preacher hitched the unhitchable Big Daddy to anybody so Kathleen's pa who's less than a dozen years older than Big Daddy kept lit the torch Kathleen and just about everybody else carried at Bear Lake after they saw Big Daddy layin naked on those big rocks in the middle of Bear Lake where he always laid sunnin his big burly belly and butt and exhibitin his famous foreskin dick right out there on the water in almost the same spot Griz and Cub were sunk drunk as a skunk in their rubber chest waders unable to move watchin Big Daddy five feet away kickin back in his rowboat gettin a boner watchin them struggle in the bubbles burblin up their own hairy bellies and up their fuzzball chests floatin in the cool dark water on a moonlit night so bright people sat on their docks under the big trees around the lake rockin in chairs and watchin out on the still water those two curly heads spittin lakewater out of their mouths like fountains in the middle of their beards and shoutin to their pa *Big Daddy come on and rescue us* and under the moon like exposin himself to some spotlight Big Daddy leaned back in the boat and rubbed his big hands up his naked thighs fingercombin his fur and runnin his palms into the dark swirls of fur on his big chest with wet nipples that stood out lit by night stars in the clear night like a constellation over the risin sine of Big Daddy's hardenin cock that made all the voices on the shore go silent out of respect except for the crickets and a loon or two whoopin at the powerful sight of two men caught neck deep wantin for all the world to be saved by a bear god in a rowboat rubbin his big wooly belly and scratchin his most beautiful beard in all of Bear County him never shavin ever even as a growin boy so that his wavy long beard was as full as ever a beard could be and he could part it in two and wrap it around his starry nipples or lean over as he did that famous night and wrap his beard around his big uncut cock which if truth be known he could suck himself better than anyone else includin Kathleen or her pa or even Griz or little Cub who all had their turns by choice or by force which was one of the stern ways Big Daddy had of makin sure everyone who turned an admirin glance on his broad hairy shoulders and the hams of his furry forearms and the baseballs of his downy biceps got a taste of his dick first in the mouth and then sized up the ass which impressed one and all becuz of the bristly bush surroundin the root of Big Daddy's blue-veined ramdick with the

uncut head slidin out so big and shiney even that night
drownin out in the middle of Bear Lake Griz and Cub who
was both themselves famously endowed thanks to their
pa had to comment at the size of their Big Daddy's huge
bear meat weighin itself maybe a pound or two and tentin up like a big white pole out of the hills of his thighs
over his shaggy pair of bear balls bouncin against his
sweet smellin butt crack and archin up the forest hills
of his belly and mountains of his meaty chest all of him
oiled with bear grease so he shined shined shined in the
moonlight on the water while Cub started to sob in his
curly beard floatin on the water cuz his big dick was
gettin bigger and harder inside his rubber waders an he
couldn't get at it and Griz was pleadin *Come on Big Daddy we need rescuin* and Big Daddy's only response was a
big bellylaugh which growled like a roar echoin through
the warm night makin all the busybody eyes watchin
from shore all the more surprised when the two hundred
and fifty fucky pounds of Big Daddy like the Lord of the
Bears stood up in the rowboat stark naked and shinin
with grizzly grease settin starlight tweakin off his nipples like lightnin rods takin a huge piss aimed right down
into the mouths first one and then the other of his two
sons who opened their faces like two little bears hungry
and thirsty for Big Daddy's big piss which was their reg-
ular drink anyway like I say about Big Daddy and the
way he trained his two boys Griz and Cub to waste not
and want not by learnin to drink his piss and lick his hair
and toothcomb his beard and tonguesuck out the sweat
from his armpits and big hairy balls and even when they
was all drunk enough which was not as often as they
pretended because pretendin to be drunk gave them

huntin permits even Bear Lake was not used to when both Griz and Cub would wrestle naked and hairy at night on the cabin floor in front of the fire so the winner could be the first one to crawl up to Big Daddy's big hard butthole and suck wind from the cave when Big Daddy hung his buttcheeks and balls over the edge of the bunk showin his big cock standin up hard with excitement and strokin it himself in anticipation of leanin forward and suckin his own big knob while Griz and Cub took turns feastin on the just desserts of his big bear belly pushin peanut butter and jelly out of his hole and them goin shit for brains nuts suckin and jackin themselves and chewin out Big Daddy's gifts of nature which of course made them see stars and howl at the moon like they was doin that famous summer night the boys thought they'd nearly drown with Big Daddy standin over them pissin down on them with them drinkin every drop and beggin Big Daddy to do with them what he wanted because he was their Big Daddy and they loved him so much and that's what Big Daddy wanted to hear so he saved them yes saved them both by cuttin them out of their rubber waders so they floated to the surface of Bear Lake and Big Daddy took ahold of them by their hair and beards and nipples and dicks and buttholes and pulled both them boys into his rowboat where they sat the rest of the night laughin and drinkin and shoutin through their beards at the moon while stars glistened between them nipple to nipple with comets shootin flume tails from their dicks and they floated ever so happy on the still surface of the water while the real constellation of the Bear rose and set over their heads and their fudgey fingers sticky from their buttholes were all entwined in the fur on their chests and the hair of their bellies and the carpet on their shoulders and the bush of their crotches and the hugeness of their beards and the curly sweep of the hair on their heads and they were all three of them so satisfied that the summer night smiled and half asleep in each other's big furry arms, Griz and Cub and Big Daddy drifted slowly across the mirror of stars to their dock on Bear Lake as if the rowboat knew their way home.

2 AM. Channel 69 **Late Show.** *Masterslave Theater* **(CC)** ★★★★*Buck's Bunkhouse*-**Drama**
Outlaw cowboy Buck Foucault (Buck Ford) discovers "what you're looking for is looking for you" when he meets existential Rancher (Bob Nevada) who changes Buck's mind about serving–as all men must–the Ultimate Master.

TV
X

BUCK'S BUNKHOUSE DISCIPLINE
THE SCREENPLAY

TWO CHARACTERS: BUCK AND THE RANCHER

BUCK FOUCAULT is a cowboy, 32, roving from ranch job to ranch job. He is good-looking and hung big so most men come on to him to admire him, but he wants more. He smokes big cigars and is attractively masculine. He wears brown leather chaps, an outback range slicker, roping gloves, and cowboy boots. He has Buffalo-Bill-length blond hair, a rugged blond beard, and a very hairy chest and belly. His blue eyes are slightly walleyed giving him a shifty look—something like a secret cocksucker who works ranches to prowl the bunkhouses in search of cowboy ass to eat. When he isn't a top hand, he doesn't mind a good bunkhouse rape of his hole by a gang of cowboys. His secret is that his nipples seduce him when men work them and he can't help himself begging for sex.

Besides the smell and feel of leather, and some really sweaty dirty sex, Buck has a weakness for cowboys and ranchers who tie him up, put a noose around his neck, and make him beg for sex.

THE RANCHER manages his own spread with emphasis on *corporal punishment*. He's mid-forties, bearded, a very disciplined loner who hires his cowboys for the actual work they can do by day—and the kind of hard-brawling balling they can do by night. He smells like a man packing a long, thick, uncut dick veined with veins as big as the veins on the backs of his big meaty hands. Showers are on Saturday nights. He runs a tight bunkhouse where the sweaty hands sleep in their stained longjohns—after many a good night of telling tall tales of their sexploits. They horse around daring each other in their cowboy gear to sniff pits, eat butt, suck cock, and fuck ass over a special brown leather Flannery Saddle. He travels twice a year to rustle up a cache of big seegars he himself smokes and gives out to his cowboy crew. He runs his ranch with the kind of corporal discipline it takes to make wild cowboy vagrants toe the line. His past is mysterious with a suggestion he knows the "real" rumors of Texas Aggies' initiations. He wears a thick black beard, maybe to mask his face, because he's got an outlaw cast to his eyes which are very intense. Cowboys who work for him may move on, but most of them come back to visit him, to get just one more taste of his man-to-man discipline they can't live without. Only two or three of such drifting cowboys have never been seen again. He wears tight jeans, a red shirt, and a cowboy hat on which he smears the cum of the cowboys he ties up, disciplines, and milks sometimes by hand and sometimes by a specially adapted stainless steel milking machine that knows no mercy. He is one of a secret group of rancher sadists all over the west who are, some bunkhouse trail-talk says, more interested in the cowboys they herd than the cattle they herd.

EXTERIOR. PALM DRIVE RANCH. THE BARBED WIRE FENCE LINE. A SPRING AFTERNOON.

LONG SHOT begins on Buck in full cowboy gear and black cowboy hat, walking the barbed wire fence line, carrying his .22 rifle. The **CAMERA TIGHTENS SHOT** as Buck approaches the camera and spits. The **SOUND** is of a lonesome cowboy singing, "O Bury Me Not on the Lone Prairie," then blends to the natural sound of the wind. Buck leans against the fence, puts the butt of his rifle in his bulging crotch, and strokes his gun barrel with his gloved hand, erotic, slow, obviously thinking bad thoughts about what he intends to pull off in the bunkhouse of his new job. He spits heavy and works his sexy mouth. His walleyed baby blues stare into the **CAMERA CLOSE SHOT** that registers him as the kind of a cowboy men would gladly buy a shot of whiskey in some two-stepping bar.

LONG SHOT. CAMERA SHOOTING UP HILL INTO SUNLIGHT THAT TURNS BUCK INTO AN ALMOST FANTASY SILHOUETTE AGAINST THE BRIGHT SKY. Buck walks his bowlegged cowboy walk, rifle on his shoulder, long slicker coat flapping around his legs until he strides strongly by the **CAMERA**.

MEDIUM SHOT. WOODPILE UNDER THE PINE TREES. Buck sets himself down, works his rifle, puffs on his big cigar, and pounds on his bulging blue-jean crotch repeatedly anticipating the rough-and-tumble cowboy sex he wanders the west to find. **CLOSE SHOT**. **CAMERA** moves around Buck, sucking up the size of his big blond build. **SERIES of CUTS** to eat up his beard, his eyes, his Brad Pitt lips, his big shoulders. He takes off his black cowboy hat, so the **CAMERA**, *moving like the viewer's eye*, can **nose** in through his blue cigar smoke and sniff his medium-long blond hair and get a whiff of his sweat-soaked pits and crotch and butt crack. He's so ready for sex, he hits his cigar with a hunger most men reserve for cock.

LONG SHOT. Buck leans against a tree pulling open his buttonflys. **CAMERA ZOOMS** in **TIGHT** as he works his big cock out of his jeans. His big dick is rooted in blond hair and the shaft, wrapped with thick cords of veins glows almost translucent red, the mushroom head already engorged.

EXTERIOR MEDIUM SHOT THROUGH WINDOW INTO INTERIOR OF BUNKHOUSE. The desert range is reflected in the glass and through the reflection the **CAMERA** sees Buck sitting, framed by the window, like a voyeur's dream of a sex portrait—which is the key to this screenplay. In exquisite profile, he is smoking his huge cigar and his big penis stands up in rampant display. The **CAMERA ZOOMS CLOSER** for a first look at his cowboy meat. He is alone and turning on to sweaty sex smells of the bunkhouse.

INTERIOR BUNKHOUSE. MEDIUM SHOT of Buck who has stripped off his high plains drifter coat. His balls are tied up with rawhide. They are big bull balls and his 9-inch-plus dick stands thick and tall. **CLOSE SHOT.** Buck's blue eyes fix intensely in mid sex-space as he sniffs the smells of the cowboys who have orgied in these rooms. Afternoon light streams in over him from his right. The **CAMERA** pulls back to **MEDIUM SHOT** for a **PROLONGED TAKE** of Buck who begins to speak in that kind of hypnotic sex drawl that flows from his mouth like rivers of cum from a dick head. He is masturbating rhythmically as he speaks and the **CAMERA** alternates **MEDIUM** and **CLOSE SHOTS** of his face, dick, and leather-tied balls. His cowboy boots are spread wide and his legs are wrapped tight in leather chaps. At times, the **CAMERA** moves up and down his body like a nose sniffing, like a tongue licking. He speaks his soliloquy to the "ideal" young cowboy he plans to rope and top and fuck come sundown when the ranch hands return.

BUCK
(*Speaking in a hypnotic sex rap of rising lust while jerking off with increasing intensity*)

You can bet I'm gonna lay your ass across a big bale of hay and fuck your butt. See how a cowboy rides. You know you want it, pig. Fuckin slidin my dick inside and out of your fuckin fuckhole. Fuckin piledrive your backside and get the rest of your buddies, my buddies, in the bunkhouse,

man, yeah! Fuckin pass you around, man,
like a fuckin bunkhouse bitch, man. Gonna stretch your bunghole open wide and
ready for us whenever we want, man.
Yeah, pig! Have you on your fuckin knees,
licking trail dust off my boots, all the way
up inside my filthy chaps. Clean it, man.
Fuckin lather up your tongue with the dirt
all over my boots. Shove my cock down
your fuckin throat, ram-slidin down your
throat, shootin my load of scum right down
your throat. Movin you on to my next buddy cuz I wanna see a smile on his face.
You fuckin suckin his stench. We all hit
the hay, layin in our bunks, pullin out our
dicks, man. You sittin on the floor. Us kickin back. Big old cigars stickin out of our
mouths, smoke curlin up through our
staches and beards. Reach down an grab
you by your hair and pull you up and choke
you with my stenchy socks tied noose tight
around your neck and cram my big horse
dick down your throat. Then take a horse
bit, man, a metal horse bit with leather
reins and stick it in your mouth. Then we
hog-tie you, piss on you, throw you in the
corner and make you sleep all night while
we just laugh pullin our dicks, not lettin
you cum till we stick a pistol in your mouth
an make you shoot off before we pull the
trigger. Yeah, boy. You gonna be our bunkhouse scum boy. Take one after the other

up your bunghole while that fuckin Rancher's poundin postholes down your fuckin
throat. Fuckin slam into your sweet little
butthole, pardner. Yeah, pig. You know you
want it. Fuckin spread those legs for me.
Fuckin slimy shit chute. Slammin my big
ol dick inside, fuckin pound it, watchin you
squirm and squeal. All them cowpokes ridin slapsaddle sittin on your face, makin
you lick their buttholes, and findin after
three days' ranchin them shit chutes ain't
so fresh. You eat ass while I fuckin fuck
you. Smell that stench, man. You eatin out
cowboy peanut butter. Dry and crunchy
hair in them cracks full of dingleberries.
Chow down on that cowboy hole. You know
you want to eat out them studs. Chewin
on their butts. Get em nice and clean,
comin over, and squattin square on your
face, bud. *YeeHA!* Till you clean every fuckin shit hole in this here bunkhouse. Clean
it up nice. You ain't spent a night till you
spent a night with a bunch of hands in a
bunkhouse. You'll crawl out all saddle-sore
swearin all them trail stories are sure as
shit true. Then you gonna watch. I can't
wait to poke my dick up inside plenty of
cowboy butt. Grabbin those hairy chests
and twistin the leather hell outa them
hard cowboy nipples. Man, you ain't seen
no rodeo till you see a couple of cowboys
fuckin each other's lights out. Fuckin

sweat and slime that drips between you.
Stenchy piss, man. Savin that sweat and
scum for days for sweet lickin.

CLOSE SHOT as Buck pulls out a big hunting knife and
teases its point and blade across first one of his tits and
then the other, moving the blade down and scraping his
tied-off purple bull balls with the cold steel, running the
sharp cutting edge up and down his big dick, alternating the knife in his crotch, on his hairy belly, hairy chest,
and twin tits. He shows off what he plans to do when he
catches up to his cowboy fuck, but, what is interesting
in a **TIGHT SHOT** of his face, is his passionate intensity for hard-riding mansex, and the **CAMERA** reveals
that Buck—interestingly changing character the way
some top men sometimes do—maybe gets turned on tor-
turing himself like some fretsome cowboy sitting alone
up in his room over a saloon where the action is more
cards than the fists, whiskey-cigar sex, and rough stuff
he wants. **CLOSE UP** of Buck's face. He fires up another big cigar. **CAMERA** pulls back **MEDIUM CLOSE** to
reveal a *large hunting knife* in his hand.

BUCK

Soon enough, I'll be scrapin your tits and
belly, man. First, I'm gonna show you
how I skin my cock and pull this cold
blade across my cockhead. You know you
want it. I want it. All them fuckin cowboys want it. Fuckin bunkhouse buddies
gettin nasty with each other. Stripped

down to nothin but our leathers. Nothin like the sound of chaps slappin ass. Leather slappin your ass, man. Filthy leathers. Cowboy boots that stink. Take a piss in one of them boots man and stick your face in and tip your head back makin you drink the piss and sweat and salt in that broken-in leather cowboy boot. Take some horse tack, man, and strap that boot to your face, wrap it around the back of your head. Keep your face shoved in that cowboy boot. All us guys blowing thick blue cigar smoke, makin you choke on it inside that boot till you puke. Then tie you spread-eagle on the floor and shove our boots into your balls. After a couple hours of discipline of your face inside that boot, I come over and unstrap you to feed you my raunchy butt. Shee-it. Feast down on it. Chew on the blond hair in my butthole. I kick back and make you eat it. Yeah, pig!

MEDIUM SHOT as Buck picks up horse bit and puts it in his own mouth, hitting his teeth, biting down, the reins wrapped around his hand. He pants heavily. The knife has scraped his dickhead to the sensitive side of raw, and he's ready to ride. The **CAMERA PANS SLOWLY** up from his balls and dick, across his forearms covered with blond hair, up across the tit clamps chained together tit to tit, up to his bearded face with the horse bit between his teeth. He shoves his big cigar in his mouth through the horse bit, so he is virtually gagged.

BUCK
(Driving himself)

Smoke it, fucker! Smoke it! That's it! Puff
it!

Buck's face reddens with passion. Blue smoke surrounds
his mouth, his nose, and hangs in his beard. He pulls on
the tit clamps. He bites down on the steel bit. His passion is rising. His eyes go out of focus. *This is a sex movie and he does what a sex star does best: he rides out of
the script to ad-lib his own passion. He's riding into the
dream of his own wild fantasy.* Ten times harder, he
yanks on his tits, bites the horse bit, smokes his stogie.
His huge dick throbs. He strokes the shaft harder. His
dick is two hands tall. Between the horse bit and the cigar in his mouth, he is on to the driven, *rising passion of
RODEO SEX where the cowboy becomes the horse!*

BUCK

Ride it, cowboy. Ride it! You're comin right
out of the chute! You got the bit in your
mouth, the bridle pullin your head back,
them spurs of that cowboy's boots diggin
into your sides.

The **CAMERA PULLS BACK** to a **FULL** torso **SHOT**
capturing Buck's auto-torture ecstasy.

BUCK CUMS, shoots his load, moaning, white plumes
of cum, hot seed, cattle sperm, runs down his hand.

The **CAMERA ZOOMS** into **CLOSE SHOT** of his spasming dick, then **CUTS UP** to his face, and **HOLDS**, then **PULLS BACK** to a head and crotch shot. Buck sways with passion. *Cum is everywhere!* He's moaning, breathing heavy. The tit clamps remain in place. He bites heavy onto the bit with the big cigar, both still in his mouth, his head wreathed with a cloud of cigar smoke very blue in the afternoon sunset pouring in through the bunkhouse window. Drool runs out of his mouth. Sperm-drool continues to erupt from his swollen penis with his balls tied off tight as a calf's nuts at a castration roundup.

FADE OUT

FADE IN

SAME INTERIOR BUNKHOUSE. SAME AFTERNOON. SLIGHTLY LATER. Buck sits mounted on a big saddle. A rope harness is bound tight around his chest, pecs, and tits, and part of the rope is tied around his throat and neck—suitable for suspension or hanging. His big blond dick, hard again, stands taller than the big saddle horn. A brown leather armband circles his left bicep. He obviously cannot control himself. He tweaks his nipples, groans, smokes another huge cigar, spits drool on his dick. Once again he's the castrating cowboy scraping his balls and cock, sticking the tip of his knife point into his nipples. The **CAMERA PANS UP AND DOWN** his action. Then the **CAMERA CUTS TO** Buck's butt on the saddle revealing the tightness of the rope harness. **REVERSE SHOT** of Buck's chest with tits clamped tied together and pulled upward toward the ceiling of the bunkhouse by a very heavy rope suitable for a lynching. An ominous feeling builds in Buck's face and voice as *he begins (as all men must) to suffer in earnest for some master he has yet to meet, but knows he must please through such preparations to readiness.*

BUCK

Fuckin rippin off my own tits. Aaaaugh! Jerkin my meat. Hurtin so good. Fuckin hangin by my tits from the bunkhouse roof, man, yeah, the pain!

CLOSE SHOT of rope harness constricting his big chest and shoulders. He's tied up now. He's strung together in a kind of *torturous bondage.* **CLOSE UP** of face. **MEDIUM SHOT** of face and chest. He raises his hand and pulls tension on the rope stretching his tit clamps up. He rocks in renewed ecstasy on the big saddle. *Is he the cowboy or the horse? He has become ambiguous.* He is no longer the aggressive top. *He has finally metamorphosed. His secret is revealed.* He has become a very aggressive bottom starving to be worked over when the cowboys ride home. His two-fisted cock sticks straight up.

BUCK

Gettin taken back to the fuckin bunkhouse. Gettin gang raped. All fuckin night by all them cowboy dicks. Dirty, fuckin dirty uncut pricks. Them ridin up deep inside my ass and one after the other down my throat.

CLOSE UP *as Buck's face and mouth contort in the ecstatic agony of pleasure-torture.*

BUCK

Fuckin balls bangin on my nose. All them scummy ranch hands. A big 250-pound cattleman's butt comin out and sittin on my face. Hey, spread those shit-chute cheeks and set your butt straight down on my face, wipin your butt on my stache and beard. I'll fuckin clean it out, man, fuckin stench, filth, slime. All the time with another big cowboy up my ass, fuckin poundin me deep. Yeah, uh-huh. Pile drive my ass, yeah, fuckin rapin me, yeah, rapin my blond hairy asshole. Throw your weight into me, man. Grab my head, fuckin me with your big uncut filthy bull dick. Rape my ass. Rape it, man. Fuckin horse bit tied tight in my mouth. Pull back on the reins, chokin me, breakin my neck, banging your balls against me. Slappin my butt. Chokin me. Give it to me, man. Gimme that fuckin scum and make me eat it in pain! Rape me. Yeah. *(Begs.)* Yeah, man. Rape me. Give it to me good. Fuckin tear up my insides with that big horse dick of yours. Empty those big balls into me. Shoot your scum deep inside my ass, that fuckin cowboy scum. I'm beggin you, man, to fuckin rape me.

CUT TO MEDIUM SHOT of Buck in same situation but with a look of sudden apprehension on his face. **THE RANCHER** walks into the **FRAME** and stands facing profile into Buck. He wears a red shirt. A can of Skoal is outlined in his butt pocket. He smokes a big cigar, bigger than Buck's. **CLOSE UP** of Buck's surprised face. **MEDIUM SHOT**. The Rancher takes Buck's nipples in both his hands.

RANCHER

Put your cigar in your mouth, son, and smoke it....That's a good little wrangler. I'm takin your tits, boy. They been clamped. They gonna be clamped again. Beat your meat. I want you in pain. This is my ranch, my bunkhouse, and you're a piece of range trash that drifted in here without much invitation. Rock your ass. Feel that big saddle between your legs, bouncin up against your butt in those chaps, bouncin up against your blond balls. You seem to be where you wanna be—in a fuckin bunkhouse and you're gonna get worked over, beat up, and raped. Hog-tied, huh? Rub that big dick. Hog-tied in the fuckin stinkin bunkhouse. I'm gonna fuckin hurt you. I'm gonna spend some time workin your tits cuz your tits make you crazy enough to want more and more till you maybe can't stand it anymore. Just me and a couple of my boys takin your sorry ass, working your great big tits, checkin your butt with our fists, force-feedin you—shit, yeah—cigar! Chokin you, man, gonna enjoy fuckin lynchin you, hangin you high, stretchin your neck. (Rancher puts both hands around Buck's throat. *Buck's eyes grow wide. He gets that look a man gets when his reason is overcome with his passion.*) Gonna take you, change you, make you the bunkhouse slave. You like me twisting your tits so nice and easy till I torture em real hard.

BUCK

Sir! Spread your cheeks and step across my face and stick my face inside your hairy cheesy ass. My whole face buried.

RANCHER
(Slapping Buck's face rhythmically)

Fuckin good ranch hand, keepin our assholes clean. (Slap) You be our fuckin outhouse, our trail toilet. (Slap) Cleanin up our boots and our socks we wipe our cum with, cleanin up our cumsocks with your tongue. (Slap) Pullin our wet wool socks over your face. Flickin our toe jam into your mouth open like a shootin target. (Slap) I'm gonna fuckin put that stogie permanent in your face. Tie that stogie into your mouth and smoke your fuckin hide. (Left slap. Right slap. Slug. Slug. Slug.)

CHANGE ANGLE. MEDIUM SHOT. Rancher rubs hot ash of his cigar on Buck's engorged cock while Buck, hypnotized by his captor, smokes his cigar. This **SEQUENCE** includes intense tit work capped with Buck feeling himself be lynched by the Rancher, strung up, sitting for all the ranchers and cowboys to see, sitting naked in a saddle, straddling the nervous stallion, feeling the noose pull on his neck, knowing he's about to be hanged, hung by the neck, and his dick stands up bright in the afternoon sun and taller than the saddle. The Rancher gets very serious with the cowboy.

RANCHER

Puttin this big fuckin rope around your neck, man. Gonna hang you up, stretch your neck. All them cowboys standin around in a circle watchin you hang there by your fuckin neck. Playin with your tits, makin your tits want that rope around your fuckin neck. I wanna hear you moan when I put these big ranch clamps on your nipples. Fuckin clamps chained together give me a good grip to pull your reins.

BUCK

Yeah. Oh, yeah. String me up, man. Work
my fuckin tits. Use my face and butthole.

CLOSE UP of Buck shouting. **PAN DOWN** to cigar ash
on clamped nipples. **PAN UP** to Buck's face. Rancher
takes the cigar from Buck's mouth, and from his own
mouth, and shoves both cigars together into Buck's
mouth held open with the metal bit. **CAMERA MON-
TAGE** of Buck begging the Rancher who works the cowboy over thoroughly, savaging his tits, roping his neck,
popping the bit between Buck's perfect white teeth, taking the cigars, and blowing smoke into Buck's open and
very willing humidor mouth. Much mouth-to-mouth cigar re-breathing and breath control. The Rancher runs
the rowels of a prized silver spur across Buck's chest, nipples, and mouth. **CLOSE SHOT INSERT** of Buck's blue
eyes on the cusp of freak-out passion. Buck pants. Drool
drips from his mouth held wide open by the horse bit and
bridle. **MEDIUM ROVING SHOT SEQUENCE** of
Rancher pulling reins to Buck's mouth with chain between tit clamps up over the reins so Buck can be dou-
ble-driven and broken like a horse with a tender mouth.
Blue clouds of cigar smoke float around Buck's head as
he jerks his big meat wildly, pushing his balls up against
the Flannery saddle horn. Buck begs for more. The
Rancher takes the reins which run straight from Buck's
mouth to under the **CAMERA** in **MEDIUM SHOT**. *Buck
wants more as much as he needs more.*

RANCHER

We gonna finish you off with a little neck-
tie party.

MEDIUM SHOT as once again the rope is tied around
Buck's neck, tightened, and he exhibits all the sensation
of a man hanging in the smoke-filled bunkhouse. **CLOSE
SHOT** as his **big dick shoots**! **CAMERA TILT UP TO
MEDIUM SHOT** of Buck's blond face exploding red with
orgasm. The Rancher eases his horse-cowboy down. Buck
pants in exhausted satisfaction. **CLOSE UP** of cum dripping down Buck's brown leather chaps. **CLOSE UP** of
Rancher smiling, *greasing up his big fist*. **CLOSE UP** of
Buck's face, surprised, begging both for mercy and for
more. Then follows the initial **SOUND** of the hard fucking of Buck's bunkhouse discipline. **SOUND MIX** includes background pickup of "O Bury Me Not on the Lone
Prairie."

FADE OUT

A Palm Drive Video Production
Buck's Bunkhouse
Written and Directed by Jack Fritscher
Produced and Edited by Mark Hemry
Starring Buck Ford and Bob Nevada
Feature running time: 60 minutes

ACKNOWLEDGMENTS

Acknowledgment and gratitude to the many magazine publishers and editors who have framed these stories into print over the years, and to the artists who illustrated the stories. Their roles in periodical publishing are often overlooked, underestimated, or lost to history.

TITANIC!

Finally, the forbidden gay love story of the most erotic cruise in history, featuring the Unsinkable Molly Brown, the Stoker, the Purser, and the Lovers who.... You will never forget this story ripped from the secret pages of a *Titanic* diary! *Titanic!* was first published as the cover story in *Uncut Magazine*, Volume 3 #1, September 1988. Editors: John W. Rowberry and Aaron Travis. *Titanic!* also published in *Mach* #35, March 1997, with illustration drawn by Ricky Ellsworth. Editors: Joseph W. Bean, Peter Millar, and Bob Fifield for Brush Creek Media.

Brideshead of Frankenstein Revisited

The hilarious erotic satire of the movies *Brideshead Revisited* and *The Bride of Frankenstein* follows the adventures of a bored longtime couple vacationing in Transylvania—and the young blond athlete (and one drop of sweat) who changes their lives. "Brideshead of Frankenstein Revisited" first was published in *Uncut Magazine*, Volume 2 #4, March 1988, with illustration drawn by the Hun. Editors: John W. Rowberry and Aaron Travis. "Brideshead" also published in the fiction anthology, *Best Gay Erotica 1997*, edited by Richard LaBonté, selected and introduced by Douglas Sadownick, Cleis Press, San Francisco.

My Baby Loves the Western Movies

Inside a storyteller's natural easy vernacular, uncut blond teen warrior, named "Horse Skin," raised on the lone prairie, sports a loincloth body that's a natural to the wandering cowboy "Red Beard" who shares their unnatural love of the unskinned dick of the old West. "My Baby Loves the Western Movies" was first published as "Buckskin Foreskin," *Foreskin Quarterly* #13, March 1990, with three photographs by Jack Fritscher.

Editor: Joseph W. Bean for Desmodus; also published in *Bunkhouse* #9, Autumn 1995, illustration drawn by the Hun, appearing in the same issue with Jack Fritscher's screenplay, *Buck's Bunkhouse*. Editors: Joseph W. Bean and Alec Wagner for Brush Creek Media.

CBGB 1977

Erotic encounters of a gonzo journalist in first days of Punk Rock introduce a young New York leather stud to the depths of new experiences of urban sex outside the famous CBGB club where rocker Patti Smith sang to the very young photographer, Robert Mapplethorpe. "CBGB 1977" was published in *Drummer* #21, Volume 3, March 1977, as "Punk Funk" with photographs by reporter Mikel Board. As editor-in-chief of *Drummer*, Jack Fritscher also wrote in this *Drummer* #21: "Getting Off" editorial, "Prison Blues" feature, "Astrologic" column, "Gay Deteriorata" satire, "Pumping Roger" feature, "Dr. Dick" column, and edit/rewrite of "Heavy Rap with an Ex-Con" with David Hurles, Old Reliable Studio. The prison-themed cover of *Drummer* #21 was a photograph of San Francisco pianist John Trowbridge shot by Jack Fritscher and David Sparrow in the bunkers on the Marin Headlands. Graphic design by A. Jay. Editor: Jack Fritscher for Desmodus. Publisher: John Embry.

Worship Me

Man-to-man adventures in a San Francisco YMCA toilet during the 1970's Golden Age of Sex reveal absolute masculinity as the hot melting core of gay sex before the virus. "Worship Me" was published in *Inches Magazine*, Volume 3 #6, August 1987, titled "Italian Groundhog Sees 10-Inch Shadow," part of Jack Fritscher's "True Tales" column, illustration drawn by the Hun. Editors: John W. Rowberry and Aaron Travis.

Seducing Butch

This "who's the hustler?" story is lesson number one in how a daredevil gay trickster uses a video camera to make a straight excon biker drop his jeans and his load. "Seducing Butch" was published as "Confessions: Seducing Straight Men" in *Uncut Magazine*, Volume 2 #4, March 1988. Editors: John W. Rowberry and Aaron Travis. A photographic portrait of Butch appears in the large-format photography book, *Jack Fritscher's American Men*, GMP, London, 1994, *editions aubrey walter*, 55 black-and-white photographs by Jack Fritscher. The video, *Butch: Tattooed Bearded Ex-Con Biker*, is available from Palm Drive Video. Running time: 60 minutes.

I Married an Aqua-Nymph

This *film noir* comedy, written to seduce straight men into autoeroticism, reveals a joyously comic, even campy, voice that exposes the diversity of gay sexuality as a public relations hustler falls in love with the coded transsexual of his dreams. This 1981 story gives first hint of Jack Fritscher's 1998 title for his novel, *The Geography of Women*, in its line: "She was a woman who knew the geography of a man's body." "Aqua-Nymph" was published in *Expose Magazine*, Volume 1 #3, April 1981, illustrated with a painting by Joe Zeni. Editor: Bob Johnson. This same issue contains a fantasy feature article also by Jack Fritscher.

Three Bears in a Tub

This breezy, breath-defying one-sentence campfire tale reveals how Big Daddy, the sexiest man on Bear Lake, rows out in the moonlight for a wet frolic with his sons, Griz and Cub, in a threesome so hot that the lake and the boat and nature itself transcend from literal sex to cosmic erotic essence. "Three Bears in a Tub" was published in *Bear Annual 1999, January 1999*. Editors: Scott McGillivray and Peter Millar for Brush Creek Media.

Buzz Spaulding's Training Academy

Big Man, 32, 6-4, 260#, will train, coach, groom, and feed "cub-boys" who dream of getting "big"! Inside secrets of how hairy men make themselves and each other into the massive, furry sex-daddies, called Bears. "Buzz Spaulding's Training Academy" was published in *Inches Magazine*, Volume 3 #11, January 1988, under the title, "Buzz Strangelove; Or, How My Dad Made My Dick Massive and I Learned to Love Every Inch," with an abstract illustration painted and collaged by Dan Marx. Editors: John W. Rowberry and Aaron Travis.

Buck's Bunkhouse Screenplay

Especially if you've never had the pleasure of reading a screenplay, pretend you are the star as you read the actual XXX-script of a porn video showcasing blond cowboy Buck and the Daddy-Bear Rancher who keeps him a sex toy with cigars and bondage! *Buck's Bunkhouse* was published as a screenplay in *Bunkhouse* #9, Autumn 1995, with five photographs by Jack Fritscher shot during the shooting of the video, *Buck's Bunkhouse Discipline*, Palm Drive Video, produced by Mark Hemry, directed by Jack Fritscher, 60 minutes; in this same issue also appeared Jack Fritscher's short story, "Buckskin Foreskin." Editors: Joseph W. Bean and Alec Wagner for Brush Creek Media.

All photographs by Jack Fritscher.

Hundreds of Jack Fritscher's photographs appear regularly in the gay press. He has shot the covers and center-folds for more than twenty magazines, and most recently for the book cover of James Purdy's novel, *Narrow Rooms*.

For more information,
reviews, biography,
or gay history, visit
www.JackFritscher.com

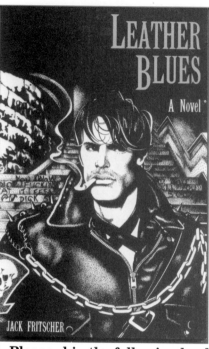

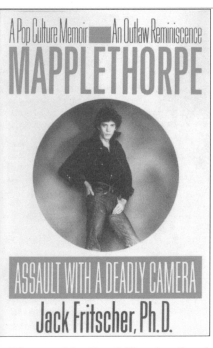

A Pop Culture Memoir ■■■ An Outlaw Reminiscence

MAPPLETHORPE

ASSAULT WITH A DEADLY CAMERA

Jack Fritscher, Ph.D.

Fritscher reveals all about his lover Mapplethorpe and their life together in NY Art Reich & PC Sex Reich!

"A passionate memoir!"
—*San Francisco Review of Books*

"reads like a juicy novel."
—*A Different Light Book Review*, NY

Fritscher on Mapplethorpe: "The Devil's Disciple"
—*The New Yorker*

"controversial...reckless!"
—*The Advocate*

"Fritscher's wild sex journals are the best roller-coaster ride in the West."
—John Calendo, *In Touch*

Please ship the following books by Jack Fritscher:

Name:_____

Address:_____

City:_____State:____Zip:_____

☐ Check here for copies signed by author
☐ *Leather Blues*, 91 pp, $9.95
☐ *Some Dance to Remember*, 562 pp, $14.95
☐ *Mapplethorpe: Assault with a Deadly Camera*, 306 pp, 32 pages of photos, $24.95 (hardcover)
☐ *Jack Fritscher's American Men*, 62 pp, 58 photos, $29.95
☐ *Rainbow County and Other Stories*, 206 pp, $14.95
☐ *Titanic: Forbidden Stories Hollywood Forgot*, 222 pp, $14.95

Sales Tax: Please add 8.5% for books shipped to CA.
Shipping: $4 for the first book and $2 for each additional.
Payment: Check/MO/Visa/MC

Card Number:_____ Exp _____

Palm Drive Publishing
PO 191021, San Francisco CA 94119
800-736-6823   Fax: 707-829-1568
EMail: orders@PalmDrivePublishing.com
See actual reviews: www.JackFritscher.com

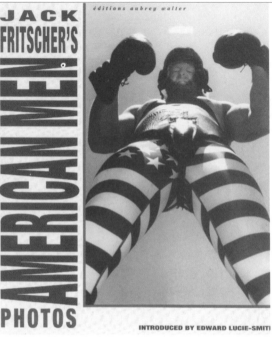

TITANIC:
Forbidden Stories Hollywood Forgot

This 4th collection of fiction by Jack Fritscher follows the National Small Press Book Award to his 3rd collection, *Rainbow County and 11 Other Stories,* as "Best Erotic Book 1998." This is author Fritscher's 12th book. In total, his books have sold to date more than 100,000 copies, and his name recognition is high from many years of publication in more than 25 gay magazines. He is best known for his biographical memoir of his life with his lover Robert Mapplethorpe, *Mapplethorpe: Assault with a Deadly Camera*, and for his epic novel, *Some Dance to Remember*, which *The New Republic* called a classic comparable to Gore Vidal and James Baldwin.

Photograph of Jack Fritscher, San Francisco 1998, by Mark Hemry